懶鬼子 英日語 Language
17buy.com.tw

懒鬼子 英日語
Language
17buy.com.tw

懶鬼子 英日語
Language
17buy.com.tw

懶鬼子 英日語 Language
17buy.com.tw

說出 美國人的 每一天

連英文老師都在學的「道地口語美語」

搭配漫畫＆圖像，
用三個步驟，學會
最道地的美式口語！

Step1 透過漫畫學習該情境常用口語

1 看漫畫學美語

在彩色漫畫中，透過兩位主角Kari及
Ivan的對話，輕鬆地學習在各個不同情
境的交談中，常用到的單字及口語。
一天一個場景，一個月後便可累積
2,000個單字、1,000句會話的實力。
並以不同顏色分別代表兩位主角，咖
啡色表Kari說的話，黑色表Ivan說的
話，清楚區分，一目瞭然。

2 重點單字及用語提示

對話中出現的重點單字或用語以黃色
標示，並將中文解釋及說明置於頁
尾。看到標示黃色的單字或用語時，
可以先測驗看看自己對該單字或用語
的理解程度，再對照頁尾的中文解釋
學習。在預習該情境對話中的重要單
字及用語的同時，加強訓練自己上下
文的連貫能力。

3 聽MP3練口說

聆聽由專業美籍錄音員錄製的MP3，跟著
MP3開口練習，用道地的美語發音說道地的
美語口語。

Step 2 透過圖像學習延伸單字及用語

1 圖解延伸單字及用語

只學漫畫中的單字及用語可不夠，每個情境單元再延伸出15-20個與該情境相關的單字及用語，並搭配生動的彩色圖像，讓你快速學習並靈活運用，說出更豐富的口語。

2 字詞庫能量值

每一個單元最後附有字詞庫能量值的檢視條，顯示到目前為止已經學會了多少美式口語中常用的單字和用語，猶如電玩中的能量值，顏色顯示的長度愈長，表示你的英文實力愈堅強！

3 聽MP3練發音

聆聽MP3，跟著美籍錄音員一起開口練習，學會延伸單字及用語的道地發音。

Step 3 來做練習吧！

重點單字或用語填空，加深印象

每個情境單元後都附有十題練習題，將前面出現過的重點單字或用語做挖空填充練習，並隨機出題，複習已學習過的重點單字及用語，加深印象，忘不了。

003

作者序

來吧，我們先把文法書放下來，用聊天的方式來學「聊天用的英文」

　　很多到過美國的朋友都曾跟我聊過一樣的問題：以前課本上背過的單字，在美國好像都各自分家，組不成句子。明明是一個簡單的生活情境，腦子裡卻擠不出相對應的形容方法；明明是常見的問答，換成美語的口語說法，就讓人思緒跟舌頭一起打結。

　　我想，這樣子的感受，不僅是在美國生活過的人才有，正在翻閱本書的你，是否也曾有過一樣的困擾呢？即使身在不用處處說英語的台灣，也有不少接觸外國人及外國文化的機會。可能在你跟外國人交談或欣賞美國影集時，聽到一個學過的字，心想：「這個字我會呢！」但突然發現，它的用法卻怎麼樣都跟課本教的搭不上邊。因為，外國人是用「聊天」的方式跟你說話，而不是用課本的教條陪你練英文。

　　在紐約求學及工作的這段期間，感受尤其深刻。紐約啊，實在不是一個學好英文的地方，但卻是一個最好學英文的精采城市。它步調快、充滿多樣性，也極具指標性。但是……

　　紐約的快，不只是步伐，還有聲調。
　　紐約的多變，不只種族，還有腔調。
　　紐約的精彩，不只生活，還有語言。
　　紐約的時尚，不只在時裝秀上，還在你每天都用得到的英文裡。

這個獨樹一格的大城市，連英文也發展出和其他城市不同的風格，紐約人特有的發音裡，帶著特有的slang（俚語），交織成美國年輕人都忍不住模仿的新口語。正因為它的創新與多變，讓它無法被一一列入英文教材裡，然而，它卻是成千上萬的美國人天天掛在嘴上的語言。

　　所以我想，比起教科書或工具書，用「聊天」的方式學英文，效果會更好、更直接。這也成了我出版本書的緣起。在書中，我設定了兩個主角人物：住在紐約的Kari和前往美國遊學的Ivan，希望透過他們在紐約各個極具指標性的景點發生的不同情境及對話，帶出美國人每一天生活中都有可能遇到的場景。跟著他們閒晃曼哈頓、布魯克林，學會在中央公園散步的時候怎麼讚嘆自然的美景；在排隊等著進餐廳的時候怎麼發洩飢餓的情緒；在商店裡廝殺血拼的時候怎麼讓店員幫上你的忙；在水泥叢林裡迷路的時候怎麼開口求救。透過兩個人的聊天對談，讓你不用花大錢出國，也能宛如置身實境般，學會各種不同場合會用到的口語！更重要的是，學會用「美國人」的方式說出來！

　　如果你希望英文能更貼近你的生活，那麼，來吧，我們先把文法書放下來，用聊天的方式來學聊天用的英文吧！

Kerra Tsai
2011.07

目錄

Chapter 1 — 各式各樣戶外活動的美式口語

在中央公園（Central Park）和上城區（Uptown）的八個景點學習戶外活動的相關用語

Chapter 4 - 其它日常生活中會用到的美式口語

在布魯克林區（Brooklyn）學習其它與日常生活相關的用語

當Kari遇上Ivan

Ivan要去紐約遊學,他在網站上找到一位住在紐約,
名叫Kari的女孩有空房分租,Ivan決定寫信聯絡她…

本書的主角

Where are you from?

I am from Seattle, USA!
我來自美國西雅圖。

How old are you?

How dare you! I am in my twenties.
你怎麼敢問？！我現在二十幾歲啦！

Very easygoing and caring!
I can be a little bossy
sometimes though.
非常好相處，而且很關心人！
不過有時候也有點霸道啦。

How do you describe yourself?

I am a movie and music buff.
我是一個電影和音樂迷。

What is your hobby?

Cheese, butter and chocolate!
Too bad they are all fattening.
起司、奶油和巧克力！不過可惜
它們都會讓人發胖。

What is your favorite food?

I am a Taurus!
我是金牛座。

How about your sign?

I have a gift for languages.
我對語言很有天賦！

What are you good at?

People like me, I guess! Those I have something
in common. 像我一樣的人吧！跟我有共通點的人。

**What type of people would
you like to be friends with?**

Hard to say! Maybe, *Funny Face* starred by
Audrey Hepburn.
很難說耶，可能是奧黛莉赫本演的《甜姐兒》。

What's your favorite movie?

South Africa, I guess! I
have always wanted to go.
南非！我一直很想去。

**If you are sponsored to travel to anywhere
you want, where is your destination?**

A bird! Flying is my ultimate dream.
鳥！因為飛翔是我最大的夢想。

**If you were an animal,
what would you be?And why?**

I am trying to be a morning
person for my health.
為了我的健康，我正努力成為一
個早睡早起的人。

**Are you a morning person?
Or a night owl?**

This is a tough one! But, yes!
I believe in fate.
這題很難，但，是的，我相信！

**Last question.
Do you believe in destiny?**

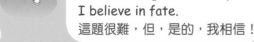

Ivan

你從哪來？（你是哪裡人？）

I come from Taipei, Taiwan.
我來自台灣台北。

你多大？

I am at the age of 22.
我今年二十二歲。

你覺得你自己是個怎麼樣的人？

My friends always say I am a pushover!
I think I just like to be helpful.
我朋友總是說我不懂得拒絕，不過我想我
只是喜歡幫助人。

你的嗜好是什麼？

Tennis is my all time favorite.
網球是我一直以來的最愛。

你最喜歡的食物？

Does cinnamon roll count?
肉桂捲算嗎？

你的星座是？

I am a Scorpion.
我是天蠍座的。

I am very detail-oriented and insightful.
我很細心而且很有觀察力。

你擅長些什麼？

Those Who I can learn from! But I don't like arrogant
people. 我可以學習的對象，但我不喜歡自大的人。

你會願意跟什麼類型的人做朋友？

Definitely *Schindler's List*.
絕對是《辛德勒的名單》。

你最喜歡的電影？

Is Mars an option too? Haha! If not,
I would say South Africa or South America.
火星也是一個選項嗎？哈哈！如果不是的話，
我想應該是南非或南美。

如果有人贊助你去旅行，那你會去哪裡？

A dog! Because dogs are
my favorite animal.
狗！因為狗是我最喜歡
的動物。

如果你是動物，會是什麼動物？為什麼？

你是早起的人？還是夜貓子？

I am a night owl! I usually
work at night time.
我是夜貓子，我通常在晚上工作。

最後一個問題，你相信命運嗎？

I think a man creates his own destiny.
我想，人可以創造自己的命運。

COOL MAN

Dear Kari,
My name is Ivan. I am from Taiwan and I plan to go to New York to study English next month.

I saw your posting on Craigslist yesterday. I want to ask you for more details about the sublease, because I am new to the city and I am not familiar with the surroundings. It is especially important to me that the location is convenient for school and general everyday needs.
Thank you very much.

Sincerely,
Ivan

凱莉，你好：
我叫艾凡，我來自台灣，下個月計畫到紐約學英文！

我昨天在Craigslist上看到你張貼的廣告。因為我對紐約不熟悉，對地理環境也不清楚，所以想問你一些有關租屋的細節。對我來說最重要的是，這個地點去學校方不方便？生活機能好不好？非常感謝！

艾凡　敬上

Hi Ivan,
WELCOME to New York, the best city in the world! I am glad that you found my posting, and I am confident that you will find this apartment to be fantastic!

Well, first of all, the subway station is just right around the corner, so it will pretty much take you anywhere you want to go in the Big Apple!And yes, I know you probably want to know this, the neighborhood is very safe. So, don't worry!

What you see on TV and in the movies can sometimes be misleading! I have lived here for 7 years and loving every minute!

So let me know if you have more questions, and again, welcome to New York, the concrete jungle where dreams are made of!

Kari

嗨，艾凡：
歡迎你來到紐約，這世界上最棒的城市！我很高興你看到了我的貼文，我很有自信你會覺得我的公寓很棒。

首先呢，地鐵站就在附近，所以不管你要到紐約的哪裡都很方便。然後呢，我想你也許想要知道這個，這是個非常安全的區域，你不需要擔心！

你在電視或電影上看到的，大多都是誤導，我已經住在這裡七年了，而且享受在這裡的每個時刻。

如果有其他問題，再請你跟我聯絡囉！再說一次，歡迎來到紐約，這個讓美夢成真的水泥叢林。

凱莉

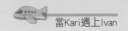

Hi Kari,
Thank you so much for the information. It was really helpful. I want to confirm the rental details with you. I am going to rent the apartment from July 13th to Sep. 13th, for $900 per month. Is it correct?

Again, I appreciate your help, and look forward to meeting you in New York City!

Sincerely,
Ivan

凱莉，你好：
謝謝你給我的資訊！幫助很大！我想要跟你確認一些租屋的細節。我想從七月十三日租到九月十三日，每個月的租金是九百元美金，這樣正確嗎？

再一次謝謝你的幫忙，很期待在紐約見到你。

艾凡

Hi Ivan,
I am so glad that you are coming! Yes, the rent and time you have listed is fine. We will handle all the paperwork once you arrive. Please let me know if I can be of help during this moving process! I know how much trouble it is to move to a new place, especially from so far away!

I look forward to your arrival as well! Trust me, you are going to love it here!

Kari

艾凡，你好：
很高興你決定要來！是的，你所列出的時間和租金都沒問題！等你抵達之後，我們再來處理文件的部分。如果在你搬過來的期間需要幫忙的話，請讓我知道！我知道搬家這件事有多麻煩，尤其還是從那麼遠的地方！

我也很期待你的到來，相信我，你會愛上這裡的！

凱莉

當凱莉遇見艾凡
When Kari Met Ivan

與人初次見面，可以這麼說：

Hi / Hello 嗨！/ 哈囉！

Hi! How are you? 嗨！你好嗎？

How do you do? 您好！

Good day. 你好！

Good morning. / Good afternoon. / Good evening.
早安。/ 午安。/ 晚安。

Nice to meet you! 很高興認識你。

Nice to see you! 見到你真好。

I'm glad to see you. 很開心見到你。

各式各樣戶外活動
的美式口語

在中央公園（Central Park）和上城區（Uptown）
的八個景點學習戶外活動的相關用語

在草地放風箏、做日光浴

Day 1 學習量：單字100個 / 會話用語35則

到綿羊草原（The Sheep Meadow）享受戶外的空氣及陽光

夏天到了，紐約也開始熱鬧了起來！今天凱莉決定帶艾凡到中央公園走一圈，好好地介紹這個紐約的後花園！首先他們來到綿羊草原。

MP3 01

凱莉：嘿，夥伴！你看，這就是我們今天的行程表。
艾凡：太棒了，看起來我們得花上一整天在中央公
　　　園裡。

凱莉：你說得一點也沒錯！
艾凡：我們可以走了嗎？

凱莉：我們到了！綿羊草原位於公園西方的中央，從六十六街到六十九街都在它的範圍
　　　內。涵蓋面積約有六萬一千平方公尺。

艾凡：它為什麼叫綿羊草原？我沒有看到任何的綿羊啊。
凱莉：如果你早個八十年來，應該就會看到了。

單字說明 ❶ 夥伴 / 好友 ❷ 深表贊同時說的話 ❸ 面積 ❹ 平方公尺

Why don't we sit down and hang out here? ①

②Fine by me! I meant to ask you actually.

艾凡：我們坐下來休息一下吧！
凱莉：我贊成，其實我早就想問你了。

Do you see the couple over there? ③ They are wearing matching-outfits. ④

And do you see the kids over there? They are flying a kite!

艾凡：你有看到那邊的那對情侶嗎？他們穿情侶裝耶！
凱莉：你有沒有看到那群小孩？他們在放風箏。

Oh my god, Kari! Is that girl taking her shirt off?

⑤Calm down, man! I think she is gonna take a sunbath. ⑥

艾凡：天吶！凱莉，那個女生在脫衣服嗎？
凱莉：冷靜一點，先生！我想她應該是想做日光浴。

With her bikini ⑦ on. Behave yourself, mister. People do that a lot.

I am not saying anything! But we are certainly in the right place.

凱莉：「穿著她的比基尼」做日光浴！別太興奮了！常常有人這樣做。

艾凡：我什麼都沒說喔！不過，我們真是來對地方了！

各式各樣戶外活動的美式口語　Chapter 1

凱莉：夠了吧！這真的是典型男生討人厭的行為。
艾凡：好啦好啦！我不說了！

艾凡：重新來過，好嗎？嘿！你看那些環繞著我們的大廈！
凱莉：那是大家喜歡來這的另一個原因，紐約的天際線。

凱莉：人們來到這，躺下，享受被這一片綠蔭包圍，然後抬頭欣賞紐約美麗的天際線。

單字說明 ❶ 失禮的行為 ❷ 理由 ❸ 仰慕／欣賞

一定要知道的**單字及用語**！

跟著Kari和Ivan逛完綿羊草原後，
別忘了繼續學習其它與本單元相關的道地美語常用單字及用語！

This is us 我們到了！
註(口語用法) 同樣也可以說：
This is me! 我家到了。/ 我到站了。

fly a kite 放風箏
The little boy is flying a kite.
那個小男生在放風箏。

Chapter **1**
各式各樣戶外活動的美式口語

meadow [ˋmɛdo] 草地
There are many children
running on the meadow.
有很多小朋友在草地上奔跑。

fine by me
我贊成 / 我沒意見
註也可以用在生氣的
時候，表示隨你便。

grass [græs] 青草
I love sitting on the grass.
我喜歡坐在草地上。

meant to ask 早就想問
I meant to ask if you are
even a student of our school.
我剛剛就想問，
你到底是不是我們學校的學生？

with... on 穿著 / 戴著
He is sleeping with his glass on.
他戴著眼鏡就睡著了。

wear [wɛr] 是指穿著的狀態
She is wearing my red dress.
她穿著我的紅色洋裝。

put on 是指穿上的動作
I am putting my coat on.
我正在穿我的外套。

spend [spɛnd] 花時間 / 金錢
I spend 2 weeks on this presentation.
我為了這場報告花了兩個禮拜時間準備。

HONEY MOON

draw up 擬定
He draws up a plan for their honeymoon.
他為他們的蜜月旅行訂了一份計畫。

OK!

typical [ˈtɪpɪkl] 典型的
This is a typical syndrome of swine flu.
這是豬流感的典型症狀。

knock it off 夠了吧!

Knock it off!
You have gone too far.
行了吧!你已經太過分了。

behave yourself 放尊重點

Kids, behave yourself!
You are out of control.
孩子們!安分點,你們快失控了。

behavior [bɪˋhevjɚ] 行為

I apologized for my son's behavior.
我為我兒子的行為道歉。

 clean slate 既往不咎

I know I was wrong about you! You have my apology. Clean slate.
我知道是我誤會你了,我道歉!重新來過,好嗎?

 I'll drop it 不說了 / 就此打住

If you don't want to talk about that, I'll drop it.
如果你不想聊,我會就此打住。

來做練習吧！Let's practice

學習完本單元的單字及用語後，趕緊來做些練習，加深印象。

① Kids, _____ _____ ! You are out of control.

孩子們！安分點，你們快失控了。

② _____ her bikini _____ . People do that a lot.

「穿著她的比基尼」做日光浴！常常有人這樣做。

③ Why don't we sit down and _____ _____ here?

我們坐下來休息一下吧！

④ _____ _____ _____ ! This is the typical social faux pas

for a guy.

夠了吧！這真的是典型男生討人厭的行為。

⑤ The little boy is _____ _____ _____ .

那個小男生在放風箏。

⑥ If you don't want to talk about that, _____ _____

_____ .

如果你不想聊，我會就此打住。

⑦ _____ _____ , okay? Hey, look all the buildings around us!

重新來過，好嗎？嘿！你看那些環繞著我們的大廈！

⑧ They are wearing _____ .

他們穿情侶裝耶！

⑨ He _____ _____ a plan for their honeymoon.

他為他們的蜜月旅行訂了一份計畫。

⑩ _____ _____ , man! I think she is gonna take a sunbath.

冷靜一點，先生！我想她應該是想做日光浴。

解答

1. behave yourself 2. With / on 3. hang out
4. Knock it off 5. flying a kite 6. I'll drop it
7. Clean slate 8. matching-outfits 9. draws up
10. Calm down

來當追星族

在草莓園（Strawberry Fields）追思永遠的偶像約翰藍儂

結束了綿羊草原的愜意，兩人繼續前進到另一個著名的景點 —— 草莓園！全世界樂迷瞻仰約翰藍儂的地方……

MP3 02

Get up, lazy bone[1]! We should get going to the next destination.

All rightly! I was almost [2]falling asleep.

Have you ever heard of the song "Strawberry Fields Forever?"

Are you joking me? The Beatles.

凱莉：起來了，你這個懶骨頭！我們應該要出發往下一個目的地去了！

艾凡：好啦好啦！我剛剛都快睡著了。

凱莉：你有聽過「永遠的草莓園」這首歌嗎？

艾凡：你開我玩笑啊？披頭四啊！

[3](humming) Living is easy with eyes closed, misunderstanding all you see. It's getting hard to be someone but it all works out. (lyrics)

Where we are standing is called Strawberry Fields, the [4]Memorial to John Lennon.

艾凡：（哼著歌）視而不見，生活會顯得比較容易，隨意誤解所見的一切。要有所作為是如此的艱辛，但船到橋頭自然直。（歌詞）

凱莉：我們現在站的地方，就叫做草莓園！是為了紀念約翰藍儂而建的。

His wife, Yoko Ono, [5]contributed $500,000 to renovate Strawberry Fields in[6] memory of him.

I am touched! Do you know why people put flowers and candles on that circle?

凱莉：他的太太，小野洋子，捐了五十萬美元，重新整修草莓園來紀念他。

艾凡：我覺得很感動！你知道為什麼那麼多人放鮮花和蠟燭在那個圓圈上嗎？

單字說明 ❶ 懶骨頭 ❷ 睡著 ❸ 哼歌 ❹ 紀念碑／紀念 ❺ 貢獻／捐獻 ❻ 紀念……

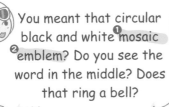 You meant that circular black and white mosaic① emblem② ? Do you see the word in the middle? Does that ring a bell?

 "Imagine," the title③ of one of Lennon's most famous song.

 Exactly! John Lennon's fans came here from all over the world to honor④ their greatest singer-songwriter.

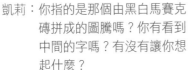 IMAGINE

凱莉：你指的是那個由黑白馬賽克磚拼成的圖騰嗎？你有看到中間的字嗎？有沒有讓你想起什麼？

艾凡：「想像」，約翰藍儂最有名的一首歌。

凱莉：正是！約翰藍儂的歌迷從世界各地來到這裡瞻仰他們心目中最偉大的歌手和創作人。

 I know that every year on Dec. 8th, his fans gather to show their outpouring of love for John Lennon.

Yes, right in this very⑤ place.

艾凡：我知道每年的十二月八號，他的樂迷們都會集合在一起表達對約翰藍儂的愛。
凱莉：沒錯，就在這個地方。

單字說明　❶ 馬賽克的　❷ 圖騰／象徵　❸ 標題／頭銜　❹ 致敬
❺ very 在此做為強調，強調「就在此地」！

凱莉：除此之外，草莓園所在地就在約翰藍儂和小野洋子所住的達可答公寓的對面。

艾凡：這樣一來，小野女士就可以每天從住所遙望草莓園。

凱莉：草莓園在一九八五年十月九號完成開放，
　　　現在已成為紐約市觀光客朝聖的景點。

艾凡：希望這位偉大的巨星以及充滿影
　　　響力的和平擁護者，長眠安息。

  ❶ 在……的對面 ❷ 為（建築物）舉行落成典禮 ❸ 朝聖地

一定要知道的**單字**及**用語**！

跟著Kari和Ivan逛完草莓園後，
別忘了繼續學習其它與本單元相關的道地美語常用單字及用語！

compose [kəm`poz] 作曲 / 寫文章

He has composed 50 songs by the age of 20.
他在二十歲之前就已經做了五十首曲子。

band [bænd] 樂團

He plays drums in his band.
他在他的樂團裡負責打鼓。

lyric [`lɪrɪk] 歌詞

I was carried away by the beautiful lyrics.
我沉醉在那美麗的歌詞中。

touched [tʌtʃt] 被感動 / 感到很感動

I was touched by the movie.
這部電影讓我很感動。

bouquet [bu`ke] 花束

I bought a bouquet of flowers for
Mother's day.
我買了一束花慶祝母親節。

gather [`gæðɚ] 聚集

We gather here for solving the problem.
我們今天聚在這裡，是為了解決問題。

advocate [ˋædvəkɪt] 擁護者 / 提倡者

They are advocate of female rights.
他們是女權的倡導者。

have influence over 對誰有影響力 （小補帖）

Lady Gaga has influence over the young generation.
女神卡卡對年輕一代很有影響力。

assassinate [əˋsæsɪnͺet] 暗殺

John Lennon was assassinated by his fan.
約翰藍儂被他的樂迷暗殺。

influential [ͺɪnfluˋɛnʃəl] 有影響力的 （小補帖）

Ted is an influential boy in his class.
泰德在班上是個有影響力的人。

activist [ˋæktəvɪst] 行動主義者 / 激進主義份子

The activists are arrested by local police.
那些激進份子被當地的警察逮捕了。

destination [ˌdɛstəˋneʃən] 目的地

Our next destination is South Africa.
我們的下一個目的地是南非。

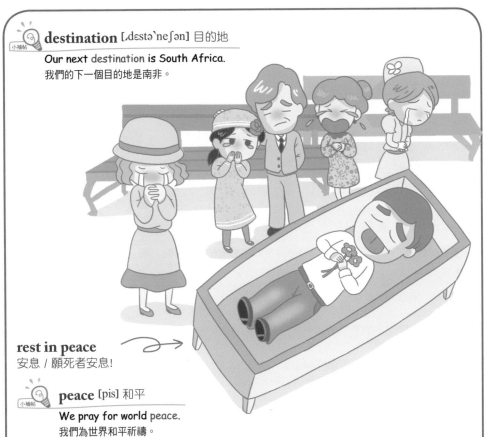

rest in peace
安息 / 願死者安息!

peace [pis] 和平

We pray for world peace.
我們為世界和平祈禱。

renovate [ˋrɛnəˌvet] 重做 / 整修

He is renovating his kitchen again.
他又再整修他的廚房了。

ring a bell 想起來

A:Do you remember Tom?
　The guy who runs a bakery!
B:Doesn't ring a bell.

A：你記得湯姆嗎？有一間麵包店的那個！
B：完全沒印象。

來做練習吧！Let's practice

學習完本單元的單字及用語後，趕緊來做些練習，加深印象。

1 I bought a _____ of flowers for Mother's day.

我買了一束花慶祝母親節。

2 I am _____ ! Do you know why people put flowers and candles on that circle?

我覺得很感動！你知道為什麼那麼多人放鮮花和蠟燭在那個圓圈上嗎？

3 All righty! I was almost _____ _____ .

好啦好啦！我剛剛都快睡著了。

4 Our next _____ is South Africa.

我們的下一個目的地是南非。

5 They are _____ of female rights.

他們是女權的倡導者。

6 Besides, Strawberry Fields is located in the Park _____ _____ the Dakota building, where John and Yoko lived.

除此之外，草莓園所在地就在約翰藍儂和小野洋子所住的達可答公寓的對面。

7 His wife, Yoko Ono, contributed $500,000 to renovate Strawberry Fields _____ _____ _____ him.

他的太太，小野洋子，捐了五十萬美元，重新整修草莓園來紀念他。

8 Yes, right in this _____ place.

沒錯，就在這個地方。

9 Lady Gaga _____ _____ _____ the young generation.

女神卡卡對年輕一代很有影響力。

10 We pray for world _____ .

我們為世界和平祈禱。

解答
1. bouquet 2. touched 3. falling asleep 4. destination
5. advocate 6. across from 7. in memory of 8. very
9. has influence over 10. peace

欣賞雕塑作品

Day 3　學習量：單字85個／會話用語30則

參觀悼念內戰的雕塑作品：畢士達噴泉（Bethesda Fountain）

結束了對約翰藍儂的悼念，兩人一路向北走，走到了畢士達噴泉，這裡是電影場景最愛取景的地方之一！

 MP3 03

I didn't know that you are a groupie! ❶

Well, when it comes to the Beatles, who isn't? ❷

凱莉：我不知道你還是個追星族咧！
艾凡：嗯……如果是披頭四的話，有誰不喜歡呢？

You know what? There are tons of movies that take place in Central Park. The place we are headed to is one of the most popular spots.

凱莉：你知道嗎？有非常多的電影都來中央公園取景喔。我們現在要去的這個地方，是最受歡迎的點之一喔！

Sounds tempting! ❸

Here we are! It's called Bethesda Fountain. A fountain with angels guarded.

艾凡：聽起來很吸引人！
凱莉：到了！這個地方叫做畢士達噴泉，一個有天使守護的噴泉。

I have read about this in my tour book. ❹ Correct me if I am wrong.

I am all ears!

艾凡：我在我的旅遊書上有讀到喔！如果我說錯的話，再請你糾正我。
凱莉：我洗耳恭聽！

單字說明 ❶ 仰慕並追隨名人的人 ❷ 說到……的話 ❸ 誘惑人的／吸引人的 ❹ 糾正

Bethesda Fountain is one of the largest fountains in NYC, and also one of the most well-known fountains in the world.

True! And the statue at its center was the first public art work designed by female artist in NYC.

艾凡：畢士達噴泉是紐約最大的噴泉之一，同時也是世界上最有名的噴泉之一。

凱莉：沒錯！而且在中央的那雕像是紐約第一個由女性設計師設計的公共藝術作品。

❶ The neoclassical sculpture, also known as Angel of Waters.

There are four small cherubim standing beneath, which representing health, purity, temperance, and peace.

Health   Purity   Temperance   Peace

艾凡：那個新古典主義派的雕像，也被稱作是水之天使。

凱莉：站在下面的四個小天使分別代表著健康、純潔、節制以及和平。

Bethesda Fountain was built in 1873 in the memory of victims from the ❷ Civil War.

I am impressed! You really did your research.

艾凡：畢士達噴泉建立於一八七三年，是為了紀念在內戰中戰死的犧牲者。

凱莉：你嚇到我了(表示對方真的有實力)，你真的有做功課耶！

單字說明　　❶ 新古典主義　❷ 內戰

艾凡：沒有啦！只是當我看到我旅遊書上的
　　　圖片時，畢士達噴泉整個就把我吸引
　　　住了。

凱莉：我相信！你看這個地方，好羅曼蒂克！

凱莉：對了！這裡同時也是拍婚紗照的熱門景點喔。
艾凡：如果我住在紐約，我一定也會在這裡拍我的婚紗！

單字說明　❶ 立即的／立刻的

一定要知道的**單字**及**用語**！

跟著Kari和Ivan逛完畢士達噴泉後，
別忘了繼續學習其它與本單元相關的道地美語常用單字及用語！

neoclassical [ˌnioˋklæsɪk!]
新古典主義的
This is a neoclassical painting.
這是一幅新古典主義的畫作。

statue [ˋstætʃu] 雕像
Have you ever been to
the Statue of Liberty?
你有去看過自由女神像嗎？

sculpture [ˋskʌlptʃɚ] 雕刻品 / 雕像
There are many sculptures
of ancient royals in the MET.
在大都會博物館裡有很多古代皇室
們的雕像。

catch one's eye 吸引……的目光
The gem ring instantly caught my eye.
那個寶石戒指一下就抓住我的目光。

cherub [ˋtʃɛrəb] 小天使
The cherubim are flying in
this picture.
這幅畫裡，小天使飛翔著。

小補帖 **be attracted by** 受……吸引
I was attracted by her elegance.
我深受她的氣質吸引。

purity [`pjurətɪ] 純潔
I admire the purity of her creations.
我欣賞她作品裡的純潔。

best man [bɛst mæn]
伴郎

groom [grum] 新郎

wedding photo 婚紗照 / 婚禮照片
She looks happy in her wedding photos.
她在結婚照裡看起來好開心。

bride [braɪd] 新娘

bridesmaid
[`braɪdz͵med]
伴娘

wedding gown 結婚禮服
I bough my own wedding gown
for the most important day of my life.
我為我人生最重要的一天，買了我自己的結婚禮服。

health [hɛlθ] 健康

Health is the greatest wealth.
健康是最大的財富。

victim [`vɪktɪm]
受害者 / 犧牲者

temperance [`tɛmprəns] 節制

Temperance of lust is very important.
對於慾望的節制非常重要。

guard [gɑrd] 守護 / 監視

The bank security guards the safe carefully.
銀行的安全人員小心翼翼地監視著保險箱。

A

B

I am all ears
洗耳恭聽

A:Do you want to know what happened last night?
B:I am all ears.

A：你想要知道昨晚發生什麼事嗎？
B：我洗耳恭聽。

小補帖 **represent** [ˌrɛprɪˈzɛnt] 代表

My boss is out of town today. I am here to represent him.
我老闆今天不在，我來代表他。

小補帖 **well-known** [`wɛl`non] 聞名的

He is a well-know basketball player.
他是一個有名的籃球員。

Chapter 1 各式各樣戶外活動的美式口語

字詞庫能量值 目前累計共學會255個單字 / 100句會話用語

❶ She looks happy in her _____ _____ .

她在結婚照裡看起來好開心。

❷ I have read about this in my tour book. _____ me if I am wrong.

我在我的旅遊書上有讀到喔！如果我說錯的話，再請你糾正我。

❸ Well, when it _____ _____ the Beatles, who isn't?

如果是披頭四的話，有誰不喜歡呢？

❹ My boss is out of town today. I am here to _____ him.

我老闆今天不在，我來代表他。

❺ I am _____ ! You really did your research.

你嚇到我了(表示對方真的有實力)，你真的有做功課耶！

❻ The bank security _____ the safe carefully.

銀行的安全人員小心翼翼地監視著保險箱。

❼ Sounds _____ !

聽起來很吸引人！

❽ I _____ _____ _____ her elegance.

我深受她的氣質吸引。

❾ _____ is the greatest wealth.

健康是最大的財富。

❿ _____ _____ ! Look at this place, so romantic!

我相信！你看這個地方，好羅曼蒂克！

解答

1. wedding photos 2. Correct 3. comes to 4. represent
5. impressed 6. guards 7. tempting 8. was attracted by
9. Health 10. I bet

大啖平價美食

在不貴也不寒酸的船屋（Boathouse），享受佐以湖光山色的平價美食

畢士達噴泉的浪漫，被一場臨時雨叫了暫停，兩人等到雨停後都餓了！到了中央公園，當然不能錯過經典的船屋餐廳，這裡不僅有湖景伴美食，還有很多經典的電影場面值得回味！

MP3 04

That's a ❶passing rain out there! Are you hungry yet?

Truth be told, I am starving!

Do you see the green house over there?

Looks like a restaurant, a very expensive one!

凱莉：剛那場雨下得真突然！你餓了沒？
艾凡：老實說，我餓扁了！

凱莉：你有看到那邊那棟綠色的房子嗎？
艾凡：看起來像是一間餐廳，而且是很貴的那種。

And a very romantic one too! Come on, our table is ❷saved!

What? I am afraid I don't have enough cash! Wait up...

凱莉：也是很浪漫的那種！走吧，我們的座位已經預留好了。
艾凡：什麼？我恐怕沒有那麼多現金耶！等等我啦……

This is the famous Boathouse restaurant. They have ❸outdoor seats where you can enjoy your meals by the lake.

You know how I would love to eat in this gorgeous restaurant. But, seriously, I have only 10 bucks and I can't let you pay for me again!

凱莉：這是船屋餐廳，很有名喔！他們有戶外的座位，你可以在湖邊享受你的佳餚。
艾凡：你知道我有多想在這裡吃飯，不過，認真的，我只有十塊錢，而且我不會再讓你幫
　　　我出錢！

單字說明 ❶ 突然下的雨 ❷ 已預留的 ❸ 戶外的

❶ Easy, easy. Believe me, 10 bucks is more than enough.

(Kari is taking Ivan to the other side of the restaurant)

凱莉：放輕鬆嘛！相信我，十塊錢很夠了！(凱莉帶著艾凡往餐廳的另一頭走去)

Here! The Boathouse ❷ express café. Not too fancy, not too shabby.

Haha, thank you, Kari! This place just hit the spot.

THE BOATHOUSE EXPRESS CAFE

凱莉：到了！船屋小吃店，不會太豪華但也不寒酸。
艾凡：哈哈！謝謝你啊，凱莉！這個地方正中我的靶心。

❸ We may not be able to savor the three courses by the lake but we can still enjoy three dollars-burger with sunshine.

Let's take out the food to that bridge. It's too beautiful to be real.

COOL MAN

凱莉：我們也許沒有辦法在湖邊細細品嚐三道菜的高級料理，但是我們還是可以在陽光
　　　下享受我們三塊錢一個的漢堡。
艾凡：我們把食物外帶到那座橋上去吧！它簡直美得不像真的。

單字說明　❶ 在此做為「放輕鬆嘛」！❷ 賣速食的小吃店　❸ 能夠(做) ……

Oh, that's Bow Bridge.

凱莉：喔！那是弓橋。

It has been a **magnificent**❶ setting in films such as *Manhattan*, *The Way We Were* and *Keeping the Faith*.

凱莉：很多電影都取它的美麗身影為景喔，像是《曼哈頓》、《往日情懷》和《相信愛情》。

Sounds like a perfect place to go!

艾凡：這樣說來，我們非去不可啦！

Bow Bridge **stretches**❷ **across** the Lake. Would you like to row a boat afterwards?

Hahahahaha, we'll see!

凱莉：弓橋橫跨了公園大湖，你等等想要來劃個船嗎？

艾凡：哈哈哈哈哈……再說吧！

一定要知道的**單字**及**用語**！

跟著Kari和Ivan逛完船屋和弓橋後，
別忘了繼續學習其它與本單元相關的道地美語常用單字及用語！

fancy [ˋfænsɪ] 很時髦的

We had dinner at a fancy restaurant last night.
我們昨天在一間很時髦的餐廳吃晚飯。

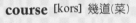

shabby [ˋʃæbɪ]
簡陋的 / 寒酸的
That bar looks shabby.
那間酒吧看起來很簡陋。

course [kors] 幾道(菜)

A formal French dinner
contains 7 courses.
正式的法國晚餐包含七道菜。

too... to...
太……以至於無法……

I am too full to eat another bite.
我太飽了，一口也吃不下了。

wait up 等我

Wait up! I hurt my ankle.
等我！我扭到腳踝了。

stretch [strɛtʃ] 伸展 / 伸直 / 伸懶腰

After a 5-hour driving, I need to stretch a little.
開了五個小時的車，我需要伸展一下。

by the lake 在湖邊
by+地方 在……旁邊
by+時間 在……之前

truth be told 老實說
Truth be told, I was never good at swimming.
老實說，我一向都不太會游泳。

row (a boat) 划船
I used to row when I was in college.
以前在大學時代，我會划船。

return / pay back 還(錢)

more than enough
非常足夠
Just saying thank you is more than enough.
只要說謝謝就夠了。

pay for someone 幫誰付錢
I don't want you to pay for me!
我不想要你幫我付錢。

gorgeous [ˋgɔrdʒəs]
十分美好的 / 燦爛美麗的
The dining-room was gorgeous. 這餐廳好漂亮。

cash [kæʃ] 現金
I don't have enough cash.
Do you accept credit card?
我現金不夠，請問你們接受信用卡嗎？

BANK = CHECK
$2000
check [tʃɛk] 支票
traveler's check 旅行支票

credit card 信用卡

來做練習吧！Let's practice

學習完本單元的單字及用語後，趕緊來做些練習，加深印象。

❶ I don't have enough cash. Do you accept _____ _____ ?

我現金不夠，請問你們接受信用卡嗎？

❷ I don't want you to _____ _____ me!

我不想要你幫我付錢。

❸ That's a _____ _____ out there! Are you hungry yet?

剛那場雨下得真突然！你餓了沒？

❹ Let's take out the food to that bridge. It's _____ beautiful _____ be real.

我們把食物外帶到那座橋上去吧！它簡直美得不像真的。

❺ _____ _____ ! I hurt my ankle.

等我！我扭到腳踝了。

❻ They have outdoor seats where you can enjoy your meals _____ _____ _____ .

他們有戶外的座位，你可以在湖邊享受你的佳餚。

❼ Would you like to _____ _____ _____ afterwards?

你等等想要來划個船嗎？

❽ _____ _____ _____ , I was never good at swimming.

老實說，我一向都不太會游泳。

❾ After a 5-hour driving, I need to _____ a little.

開了五個小時的車，我需要伸展一下。

❿ That bar looks _____ .

那間酒吧看起來很簡陋。

解答

1. credit card 2. pay for 3. passing rain 4. too / to
5. Wait up 6. by the lake 7. row a boat
8. Truth be told 9. stretch 10. shabby

048

排隊拿免費戲票

Day 5 學習量：單字70個 / 會話用語30則

去戴拉寇特戲院（Delacorte Theater）排隊領免費的票，欣賞莎翁名劇

在美麗的弓橋邊飽餐一頓之後，兩人又繼續向北走，突然眼前出現一大片人海，艾凡很驚訝，凱莉卻好像早有準備！原來他們的下一站就是「戴拉寇特戲院」，這劇院最為人津津樂道的就是每年夏天免費演出的莎士比亞劇，現在，一起排隊拿免費的票吧！

MP3 05

凱莉：你有看到那邊那些人群嗎？那就是我愛紐約的原因。

艾凡：怎麼說？他們在等什麼？

凱莉：免費的莎士比亞劇票。

艾凡：不可能！不要什麼都不跟我說嘛！

凱莉：戴拉寇特戲院最廣為人知的就是每年夏天所製作的莎士比亞劇。

艾凡：那戲院在哪裡？

單字說明　❶ 怎麼說　❷ 對……隱瞞　❸ 夏日的

It is located at the heart of Central Park. The Theater itself is an open-air theater. Both Turtle Pond and the majestic Belvedere Castle can be seen in the background.

凱莉：就在中央公園的核心，劇院本身是個開放的戶外劇場。烏龜池和望景城堡都是演出時的背景。

Unbelievable! Watching Shakespeare's play in an ❶open-air theater in Central Park! The coolest thing ever! ❷

艾凡：太不可思議了！在中央公園的戶外劇場看莎翁名劇！簡直就是人生中最酷的事！

Not to mention it is free. As long as one is prepared to ❸wait in line on the day of the performance to obtain tickets.

Just like what we are doing now.

凱莉：更別提這全都是免費的喔。只要你準備好表演當天的白天排隊等候領票！
艾凡：不就是我們現在在做的事嗎？

 單字說明　❶ 戶外的 / 開放的　❷ 在此做「有史以來」用，通常用來作誇飾　❸ 排隊等候　**051**

Can we get tickets ❶ at all?
There are already thousands
of people ahead of us.

艾凡：我們真的有可能拿到票嗎？我們
　　　前面已經有好幾千人了吧。

No worries; the theater ❷ boasts a
seating capacity of 1,872. We have
a big chance to get in.

凱莉：別擔心，這個戲院可以容納一千八百七
　　　十二個人次！我們很有機會進場的。

❸ Plus, they invite famous Hollywood
stars to perform, too. I remember
they ❹ invited Anne Hathaway in 2009.

Anne
Hathaway

凱莉：不僅如此，他們每年都會邀請好萊塢的明星來表演，我記得二〇〇九年請的是安
　　　海瑟威。

Anne?! She is my favorite.
She is intelligent, sexy,
adorable, and...

Oh, come on! ❺ I get it! Cut it off!

艾凡：安？！她是我的最愛！她又聰明，又性感而且很可愛……
凱莉：喔，拜託！我知道了！可以停了嗎？

 ❶ 用在問句有「有可能嗎？到底……」的意思　❷ 包含　❸ 更好的是　❹ 邀請　❺ 我瞭解了 / 我知道了

一定要知道的**單字及用語**！

跟著Kari和Ivan逛完戴拉寇特戲院後，
別忘了繼續學習其它與本單元相關的道地美語常用單字及用語！

capacity [kəˋpæsətɪ] 容量

The room has a capacity of 8 people.
這個房間可以容納八個人。

location [loˋkeʃən] 地點 / 位置

First thing first, give me
the location of your shop.
先辦正事，告訴我你的店在哪裡。

known for 因……而知名

The bakery is known for its
cinnamon rolls.
那家麵包店因為它的肉桂捲而聲名大噪。

be located 位於

My shop is located
within the flea market.
我的店就在跳蚤市場裡面。

小補帖 **obtain** [əbˋten] 得到

They obtain a big amount of compensation.
他們得到一筆為數龐大的賠償金。

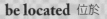

castle [`kæsl] 城堡

Many fairy tales start with a princess locked in a castle.
很多童話故事都以被關在城堡裡的公主開場。

be prepared 準備好

I am prepared for the audition tomorrow.
明天的試鏡我已經做好準備了。

production [prə`dʌkʃən]（電影的）製作

The production of this film cost up to 100,000,000.
這部電影的製作費用超過一億元。

pond [pɑnd] 池塘

You can see fish swimming in the pond.
你可以看到魚在池塘裡游泳。

not to mention
更不用說

I don't even know him, not to mention like him.
我根本不認識他，更別說喜歡他。

plus [plʌs] 加分

He can sing well which is a huge plus.
他很會唱歌，這很加分。

各式各樣戶外活動的美式口語

Chapter 1

① The _____ of this film cost up to 100,000,000.

這部電影的製作費用超過一億元。

② _____ , they invite famous Hollywood stars to perform, too.

不僅如此，他們每年都會邀請好萊塢的明星來表演。

③ Stop keeping me _____ _____ _____ , please!

不要什麼都不跟我說嘛！

④ The bakery_____ _____ _____ its cinnamon rolls.

那家麵包店因為它的肉桂捲而聲名大噪。

⑤ As long as one is prepared to _____ _____ _____ on the day of the performance to obtain tickets.

只要你準備好表演當天的白天排隊等候領票！

⑥ Can we get tickets _____ _____ ?

我們真的有可能拿到票嗎？

⑦ I have a busy weekend _____ _____ me.

我有個忙碌的週末等著我。

⑧ I _____ _____ for the audition tomorrow.

明天的試鏡我已經做好準備了。

⑨ The theater _____ a seating capacity of 1,872.

這個戲院可以容納一千八百七十二個人次！

⑩ My shop _____ _____ within the flea market.

我的店就在跳蚤市場裡面。

解答

1. production 2. Plus 3. in the dark 4. is known for
5. wait in line 6. at all 7. ahead of 8. am prepared
9. boasts 10. is located

欣賞音樂會

到林肯中心（Lincoln Center）欣賞各式各樣的音樂饗宴

林肯中心的戶外表演開場了，這是每個紐約人每年夏天引頸期盼的盛會。林肯中心是世界上第一個將各表演藝術集合在同一場地的表演中心，除了提供優質的表演外，還提供許多免費的活動，將藝術表演深入民眾，今晚凱莉要到林肯中心與大家同樂，一起去享受音樂和熱情吧！

MP3 06

❶ (Text message)

Hey lady, are you free tonight? Would you like to go to a movie with me? My treat!

(Text message)

Thank you for asking! But I am headed to Lincoln Center for the "Lincoln Center Out of Doors."

簡訊（艾凡傳給凱莉）
嘿！今天晚上有空嗎？願不願意和我去看場電影？我請客！

簡訊（凱莉回覆）
謝謝你的邀請！但是今晚林肯中心有個叫做「林肯中心戶外音樂節」的戶外活動，我要到那裡去。

(Text message)
Okay! Never mind. Have a great night.

(Text message)
This event is my all time favorite. Love for you to come and join me!

簡訊（艾凡傳給凱莉）
好！沒關係！那你好好玩！

簡訊（凱莉傳給艾凡）
這是我一直以來最喜歡的活動！如果你也一起來參加我會很開心！

Now I know why you are so deeply in love with this city.

I know! You can never be bored in this **❷** concrete jungle.

艾凡：現在我知道你為什麼這麼熱愛這個城市了。
凱莉：就是說啊！在這水泥叢林裡你永遠不會覺得無聊。

 ❶ 簡訊 ❷ 水泥叢林，意指都市

Tell me something about this "Lincoln Center Out of Doors!"

Every August, music, dance and performance from cultures across the globe fill the plazas ❶ of Lincoln Center.

艾凡：跟我分享一些「林肯中心戶外音樂節」的訊息吧！

凱莉：每年的八月份，來自各種文化的音樂、舞蹈和表演都會充斥著林肯中心的廣場。

❷ More than 100 shows will be held through August.

And let me guess... Obviously, it is FREE.

凱莉：整個八月，將有超過一百場的表演在這裡舉辦。

艾凡：讓我來猜猜看……很明顯地，全都是免費的吧。

Certainly! How can you miss it, right?

Props to you! I am so lucky to have such a ❸savvy local like you.

凱莉：當然！所以，你怎麼能錯過呢？
　　　對嗎？

艾凡：多虧有你！我真的很幸運有你這個
　　　熟門熟路的道地紐約客。

Chapter 1

各式各樣戶外活動的美式口語

You can see various performance here in Lincoln center, such as the ballet, opera, classical music... etc.❷

凱莉：在這裡你可以看到各式各樣不同的表演，像是芭蕾啦，歌劇啦，或是古典音樂…
……等等。

Is that Juilliard School, one of the best music institutes in the world?

Yes it is! One of the facilities, Alice Tully Hall, is located within❸ the Juilliard School building. If you are interested in the performance schedule, you can look into it online.

艾凡：那是茱莉亞學院嗎？那個世界知名的音樂學院？
凱莉：是的！林肯中心的其中一棟表演廳「艾莉絲杜麗廳」就位在茱莉亞學院裡。如果
你對表演的節目表有興趣的話，你還可以上網查相關資訊喔！

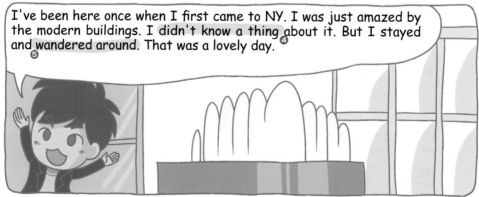

I've been here once when I first came to NY. I was just amazed by the modern buildings. I didn't know a thing about it.❹ But I stayed and wandered around.❺ That was a lovely day.

艾凡：我剛到紐約的時候有來過這裡一次，當時只是驚豔這裡摩登的建築。我根本不
知道林肯中心是什麼，不過我留在這裡到處晃了晃！那真是美好的一天！

  ❶ 像是 ❷ (et cetera) 等等 ❸ 在……裡面 / 在……之中 ❹ 什麼都不知道 ❺ 到處閒晃

一定要知道的**單字及用語**！

跟著Kari和Ivan逛完林肯中心後，
別忘了繼續學習其它與本單元相關的道地美語常用單字及用語！

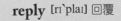

各式各樣戶外活動的美式口語 Chapter 1

reply [rɪˋplaɪ] 回覆

I emailed her last week, but she hasn't replied me yet.
我上禮拜有寄電子郵件給她，
但她還沒回覆我。

text [tɛkst] 純文字檔案（因簡訊只有文字，所以text message就是傳簡訊的意思。），text可當名詞或動詞用。

I received a text message!
我收到了一個簡訊。

I'll text when I get there!
我到了會傳簡訊給你。

my treat 我請客

Let's have a feast! My treat!
吃頓大餐吧！我請客！

be in love with 愛上……

This pizza is superb; I am in love with it.
這披薩真的太好吃了，我愛上我的披薩了。

fill (with) 充滿／填滿

His mouth fills with food.
他的嘴裡都是食物。

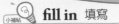

小補帖 **fill-in** 替補者　小補帖 **fill in** 填寫　小補帖 **fill out** 變胖，亦可作為填寫

look into 深入查看

Write the brand down, we can look into it online later on.
把那個牌子抄下來，我們晚點可以上網查查看。

and so on ……等等

I bought some vegetables, carrots, cucumbers, celery, and so on.
我買了一些蔬菜，有紅蘿蔔、小黃瓜、芹菜等等……。

wander vs. wonder

wander [ˋwɑndɚ] 閒晃 / 迷失

He had no idea where to go and just wandered in the street.
他不知道要去哪裡，所以就在街上閒晃。

wonder [ˋwʌndɚ]（當動詞）
納悶 / 懷疑 / 不明白
I wonder if he knows who I am.
我懷疑他知不知道我是誰。

wonder [ˋwʌndɚ]（當名詞）
驚奇 / 奇蹟 / 美好的事
His wife has done wonder for him.
他的太太奇蹟似地讓他變了一個人。

freebie [ˋfribi] 免費的東西

Why don't you take that ticket? It's a freebie anyway.
你幹嘛不拿票？反正是免費的啊！

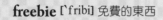

head to 前往

Where are you heading to?
你要去哪？

props to someone 多虧了⋯⋯
Props to Sue, she has arranged everything.
多虧了蘇,她把所有事都安排好了。

be amazed by 驚艷於⋯⋯
I was amazed by the fine work of her painting.
對於她畫作的精細,我感到很驚艷。

obviously [ˋɑbvɪəslɪ] 很明顯地
Obviously, you despite her!
很明顯地,你討厭她!

laid-back 悠閒的 / 無憂無慮的
I like the laid-back way he makes his life.
我喜歡他那種悠閒的生活。

小補帖 **savvy** [ˋsævɪ] 理解能力
It's always nice to have a savvy local show you around the new city.
有一個熟門熟路的當地人帶著你體驗這個新城市絕對是件好事。

各式各樣戶外活動的美式口語　Chapter 1

來做練習吧！ Let's practice

學習完本單元的單字及用語後，趕緊來做些練習，加深印象。

1 _____ _____ 100 shows will be hold through August.

整個八月，將有超過一百場的表演在這裡舉辦。

2 I bought some vegetables, carrots, cucumbers, celery, and _____

_____ .

我買了一些蔬菜，有紅蘿蔔、小黃瓜、芹菜等等……。

3 You can never be bored in this _____ _____ .

在這水泥叢林裡你永遠不會覺得無聊。

4 Every August, music, dance and performance from cultures across the globe fill the

_____ of Lincoln Center.

每年的八月份，來自各種文化的音樂、舞蹈和表演都會充斥著林肯中心的廣場。

5 Why don't you take that ticket? It's a _____ anyway.

你幹嘛不拿票？反正是免費的啊！

6 _____ _____ Sue, she has arranged everything.

多虧了蘇，她把所有事都安排好了。

7 I am so lucky to have such a _____ _____ like you.

我真的很幸運有你這個熟門熟路的道地紐約客。

8 One of the facilities, Alice Tully Hall, is located _____ the Juilliard

School building.

林肯中心的其中一棟表演廳「艾莉絲杜麗廳」就位在茱莉亞學院裡。

9 His mouth _____ _____ food.

他的嘴裡都是食物。

10 I'll _____ when I get there!

我到了會傳簡訊給你。

解答

1. More than 2. so on 3. concrete jungle 4. plazas
5. freebie 6. Props to 7. savvy local 8. within
9. fills with 10. text

熟悉適應新環境

協助剛搬到上西城區（Upper West Side）的朋友熟悉新環境
艾凡的朋友搬進了上西城區，和下城相較之下悠閒的步調，帶給上西城區另一番愜意的風味！在艾凡的要求下，凱莉列了一張上西城的餐廳推薦列表，我們也一起去嚐鮮吧。

MP3 07

艾凡：凱莉，你有空嗎？
凱莉：嗯！我有點忙耶，明天有個重要的考試！

艾凡：喔！好！我不吵你了。
凱莉：反正我也要停下來吃點東西休息一下，怎麼了？

艾凡：是我的朋友珍妮啦！她前幾天剛到紐約。她租了一個在上西城的公寓，想知道
　　　附近有沒有什麼地方好去。

單字說明 ❶ 忙得抽不開身 ❷ 打擾 ❸ a couple of 幾個…… / a couple of days 幾天

凱莉：我知道了！我可以幫她列一張表！那是一個很好的地區，她會住得很愉快的。

艾凡：謝謝你！希望不會太麻煩你！
凱莉：別傻了！完全不會！

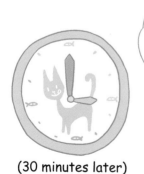

(30 minutes later)

三十分鐘以後

凱莉：嘿！我列出了一些餐廳和咖啡店喔！

單字說明　❶ 列表　❷ 煩擾／打擾　❸ 別傻了　　**067**

Cafe Lalo

Where Meg Ryan and Tom Hanks met in the movie *You've Got Mail*. This café is absolutely beautiful and delicious.

這是電影《電子情書》裡，梅格萊恩和湯姆漢克相遇的咖啡店！這間咖啡店不但非常漂亮，餐點也很可口。

Popover

"I aimed to create a warm, welcoming, comfortable atmosphere with appealing, fresh unpretentious food." said the founder. And I think she has done a great job.

「我的目標是要創造一個很溫暖，讓人感覺很受歡迎並且舒適的環境，再加上新鮮美味的食物。」創辦人這麼說。我想，她真的做到了！

Barney Greengrass

They are known for their matchless salmon and is rated the best smoked salmon in town. It may be a little pricy but it's worth every dime you spend.

他們無人能敵的鮭魚，被選為是紐約最棒的燻鮭魚，遠近馳名！也許價格不是那麼可愛，但是你花的每一分錢都是值得的。

French Roast

Every time I pass by, this restaurant is full of people. French Roast is open 24 hours daily providing the lively atmosphere of a Parisian bistro.

每次我經過這家店，總是坐了滿滿的人。它天天二十四小時營業，提供巴黎餐館特有的活力。

Jean George

Though it is a Michelin 3-star restaurant, it offers a lunch special for you to savor the delicacies with an affordable price.

雖然這是一間米其林三星級的餐廳，但他提供特價午餐，讓你荷包不失血也能享受珍饌。

 ❶ 樸實的 / 不矯作的 ❷ 被評為 ❸ 經過 ❹ Michelin 米其林（法國知名輪胎製造商米其林公司為促進汽車旅遊而發起的旅遊資訊評價，針對全球各地的餐廳及旅館以三星級評等機制做評鑑，現已成為頗具權威及代表性的美食及旅遊指南）❺ 細細品嚐

一定要知道的**單字及用語**！

跟著Kari和Ivan逛完上西城區後，
別忘了繼續學習其它與本單元相關的道地美語常用單字及用語！

tied up 忙到無法抽身
I am tied up in office, will be about 15 minutes late.
我在辦公室裡忙到沒辦法離開，可能會遲到十五分鐘！

tie [taɪ] 綁
Wait up! I need to tie my shoelaces.
等等！我要綁鞋帶。
My hands are tied.
我無能為力。

list [lɪst] 表 / 列表
I make a list of what I can't eat during pregnancy.
我列了一張懷孕期間不能吃的東西的列表。

aim to 以……為目標
I aimed to win this competition.
我以獲勝為目標。

snack break 點心時間
（snack 小零食；小點心 / break 休息時間）
Is it okay if I have a snack break? I haven't eaten all day.
我可以吃個點心休息一下嗎？我今天都還沒吃東西。

anyway [ˋɛnɪͺwe] / **anyhow** [ˋɛnɪͺhaʊ]
反正 / 不管怎樣 / 無論如何
Anyway, I have made my decision.
不管怎樣，我已經做好決定了。

lease [lis] 租約 / 契約

Can we say next Tuesday to sign up the lease?

我們可以約下禮拜二來簽約嗎？

rent [rɛnt]（當動詞）租

I rent a single house next to my parents' place.

我在我爸媽家旁邊租了一間公寓。

rent [rɛnt]（當名詞）租金

I spend 1/3 of my salary for my rent.

我三分之一的薪水都拿來付房租了。

sublet [sʌbˋlɛt] 轉租

My friend will go to Europe for 3 months, so that I sublet her apartment in NY.

我朋友要去歐洲三個月，所以我轉租了她在紐約的公寓。

Do you mind if I sit here?

你介意我坐在這嗎？

not at all
完全不會

Not at all.
完全不會。

appealing [əˋpilɪŋ]
有魅力的 / 動人的
Joan is an appealing girl.
瓊是一個很有魅力的女孩。

matchless [ˋmætʃlɪs] 無人能敵的
Vera Wang's wedding gowns are matchless.
王薇薇的婚紗禮服無人能比。

atmosphere [ˋætməsˏfɪr] 氣氛
The atmosphere in this restaurant is very cozy.
這家餐廳的氣氛非常溫馨。

delicacy [ˋdɛləkəsɪ] 美味佳餚
Truffle and caviar are both delicacies.
松露和魚子醬都是精緻佳餚。

Tapas 西班牙小菜

bistro [ˋbistro] 小酒館 / 小餐廳
Why don't we go to the French bistro at the corner?
我們去轉角那間法國小酒館吧！

lunch special 特價午餐
Many high-end restaurants offer lunch special.
許多高檔餐廳都有提供特價午餐。

來做練習吧！Let's practice

學習完本單元的單字及用語後，趕緊來做些練習，加深印象。

❶ Don't let me _____ you.

別讓我打擾到你了。

❷ Can we say next Tuesday to sign up the _____ ?

我們可以約下禮拜二來簽約嗎？

❸ Truffle and caviar are both _____ .

松露和魚子醬都是精緻佳餚。

❹ Well, I am kind of _____ for the big test tomorrow.

嗯！我有點忙耶，明天有個重要的考試！

❺ Everytime I _____ _____ , this resturant is full of people.

每次我經過這家店，總是坐了滿滿的人。

❻ Don't be silly! _____ _____ _____ .

別傻了！完全不會！

❼ The _____ in this restaurant is very cozy.

這家餐廳的氣氛非常溫馨。

❽ I _____ _____ win this competition.

我以獲勝為目標。

❾ I see! I can _____ _____ _____ for her!

我知道了！我可以幫她列一張表！

❿ Is it okay if I have a _____ _____ ? I haven't eaten all day.

我可以吃個點心休息一下嗎？我今天都還沒吃東西。

解答

1. interrupt 2. lease 3. delicacies 4. tied-up 5. pass by
6. Not at all 7. atmosphere 8. aimed to 9. make a list
10. snack break

吃下午茶、逛博物館

Day 8 學習量：單字75個 / 會話用語35則

去上東城（Upper East Side）享受下午茶，逛大都會博物館

紐約市區中最高級的地段，精品店、高級住宅區的集中地——上東城，也是影集花邊教主（Gossip Girl）中各大主角從小生長的環境！來到這，絕不能錯過紐約最引以為傲的博物館：大都會博物館、古根漢博物館、惠特尼博物館，和高級餐廳！

MP3 08

> Hey, I am home! It's muggy outside! What are you on now?

> Gossip Girl! All of my friends in Taiwan are talking about this drama. ❶

凱莉：我到家了！外面又悶又熱！你在幹嘛？
艾凡：看影集《花邊教主》啊！我台灣的朋友全都在討論這部戲。

> Keep going. Don't stop on my account.

> I was about to ❷ stop right here! I just can't stand ❸ all that scheme and twisted plots.

凱莉：繼續看啊！別因為我停下來。
艾凡：我本來就打算要在這裡停下來了！我真是受不了那些勾心鬥角和扭曲的情節。

> Well... I don't know much about ❹ either Gossip Girl or Upper East Side. Lady M, Serendipity and Kai may be the only three things I know.

> Let me guess... they are all restaurants, right?

凱莉：嗯……不管是花邊教主還是上東城的生活我真的都不太瞭解！我唯一知道的就是「Lady M」、「Serendipity」和「Kai」了吧！

艾凡：讓我來猜猜看！這些全都是餐廳，對吧？

 ❶ 戲劇 ❷ 本來就打算要…… / 原本打算要…… ❸ 忍受
❹ 不僅是…… / 連……也(不)，either 是否定的連接詞

❶ You know me well! Speaking of Lady M, they make the crepe to die for!

I kind of feel like the frozen hot chocolate from Serendipity.

凱莉：你真瞭解我！說到「Lady M」他們家的千層蛋糕真的非常好吃。

艾凡：我對「Serendipity」的熱巧克力冰沙還比較有興趣。

Paper, rock, scissors?

Deal! Bring it!

凱莉：那猜拳吧，剪刀、石頭、布。
艾凡：一言為定，放馬過來吧！

Okay. I guess it's your call! ❷

Then frozen hot chocolate it is. What else can we do in the Upper East Side?

凱莉：好吧！你決定吧。
艾凡：那就是熱巧克力冰沙獲勝啦！我們在上東城還可以做些什麼？

各式各樣戶外活動的美式口語　Chapter **1**

單字說明　❶ 說到（speaking of the devil 說到曹操，曹操就到）❷ 你決定

We don't even have to do anything. Just walking on the street would be a great pleasure. But if you insist, the MET is where I highly recommend.

凱莉：其實不需要做什麼，我覺得走到上東城街上就很享受了！不過如果你堅持的話，
　　　我相當推薦大都會博物館。

I am not a big art fan though. Besides, why should I pay the ticket for something I don't care for? ❶

(frown) I hate it when you say so!

艾凡：我對藝術沒有很大的興趣耶，而且，我幹嘛要花錢買票去看那些我不喜歡的東西？
凱莉：（皺眉）我真的很討厭你這樣説。

You can donate 1 dollar for a free entrance to the MET.

Really? A ❷ dollar won't kill me, now I am now up for ❸ an art trip.

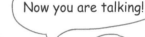

Now you are talking!

凱莉：你只要捐個一塊錢，就可以免費入場了。
艾凡：真的喔？一塊錢不算什麼！現在我想要來
　　　個藝術之旅了。

凱莉：終於説了點人話了你！

 ❶ 喜歡　❷ 沒差，不算什麼　❸ 對……有興致

一定要知道的**單字及用語**！

跟著Kari和Ivan逛完上東城後，
別忘了繼續學習其它與本單元相關的道地美語常用單字及用語！

stuffy [`stʌfɪ] 悶熱的 / 空氣不好的

It's stuffy in here! The room smells bad.
這裡面好悶熱，房間味道不太好聞。

muggy [`mʌgɪ] 悶熱

It's muggy outside, very hot and humid.
天氣很悶，又濕又熱的。

if you insist 如果你堅持的話

I will repaint the wall, if you insist.
如果你堅持的話，我會重新漆這道牆。

 小補帖 **if you have to know**

如果你非得知道不可
（有時用於被逼問而不耐煩時）
I flunked my math if you have to know!
如果你非得知道不可，我數學被當了！

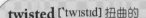

twisted [`twɪstɪd] 扭曲的

Why did you kick the poor dog? You are twisted.
你幹嘛踢那隻可憐的狗？你的人格很扭曲。

cut to the chase 言歸正傳 / 切入重點

Let's cut to the chase. I don't have time for this nonsense.

切入正題吧，我沒空聽你胡說八道。

I don't care!

shrug [ʃrʌg] 聳肩（表示無能為力、不在乎）

When I ask about what he has done, he just shrugs.

當我問他到底發生什麼事時，他只是聳聳肩。

scheme [skim] 計畫 / 詭計

This is a scheme to make him tell the truth.

這是一場為了讓他說出真相的詭計。

 小補帖 **on someone's account** 因為……誰的關係

Don't give the chance up on my account.

別因為我放棄那個機會。

Okay, I'll go to that party with you!
好吧！那我跟你一起去那個派對。

Now you are talking.
現在你總算說點好聽話了。

Now you are talking.
你總算說點人話了（在終於達成共識時說的話）

Now we are on the same page.
我們終於達成共識了

plot [plat] 情節
The plots in this novel are very boring.
這本小說的情節很無聊。

frown [fraun] 皺眉
His boss frowned on his marketing report.
老闆皺著眉看他的市場報告。

❶ All of my friends in Taiwan are talking about this _____ .
我台灣的朋友全都在討論這部戲。

❷ _____ _____ Lady M, they make the crepe to die for!
說到「Lady M」，他們家的千層蛋糕真的非常好吃。

❸ The _____ in this novel are very boring.
這本小說的情節很無聊。

❹ A dollar won't kill me, now I am now _____ _____ an art trip.
一塊錢不算什麼！現在我想要來個藝術之旅了。

❺ It's _____ in here! The room smells bad.
這裡面好悶熱，房間味道不太好聞。

❻ When I asking about what he has done, he just _____ .
當我問他到底發生什麼事時，他只是聳聳肩。

❼ Besides, why should I pay the ticket for something I don't _____ _____ ?
而且，我幹嘛要花錢買票去看那些我不喜歡的東西？

❽ I _____ _____ _____ stop right here!
我本來就打算要在這裡停下來了！

❾ His boss _____ on his marketing report.
老闆皺著眉看他的市場報告。

❿ Let's _____ _____ _____ . I don't have time for this nonsense.
切入正題吧，我沒空聽你胡說八道。

解答
1. drama 2. Speaking of 3. plots 4. up for 5. stuffy
6. shrugs 7. care for 8. was about to 9. frowned
10. cut to the chase

2

購物、參與節慶活動 &觀賞比賽的美式口語

在中城區（Midtown）的七個景點學習購物、參與節慶活動及觀賞比賽的相關用語

Unit 9 | 逛櫥窗、購物享樂
在本單元可學到90個常用單字及生活用語

Unit 10 | 參與熱鬧的節慶活動
在本單元可學到110個常用單字及生活用語

Unit 11 | 現場看籃球比賽最熱血！
在本單元可學到135個常用單字及生活用語

Unit 12 | 搭乘交通工具
在本單元可學到85個常用單字及生活用語

Unit 13 | 約會要遲到了！
在本單元可學到95個常用單字及生活用語

Unit 14 | 在戶外利用wi-fi上網
在本單元可學到110個常用單字及生活用語

Unit 15 | 登高看夜景
在本單元可學到105個常用單字及生活用語

逛櫥窗、購物享樂

Day 9 學習量：單字50個 / 會話用語40則

在購物天堂第五大道 （Fifth Avenue）血拼

為了買參加朋友婚禮的禮服，凱莉和艾凡在第五大道上廝殺了一個下午，順道參觀了美麗莊嚴的聖派翠克天主教堂，也嚐到了當地人才知道的餐車美食。

MP3 09

I am ❶ in search of a dress for a friend's wedding! Let's go shopping!

No problem! I think Fifth Avenue is the best place to go.

凱莉：我要找一件可以穿去朋友婚禮的洋裝，你陪我去挑吧！
艾凡：好啊！那第五大道想必是我們的最佳去處。

You can find not only the high-end designer brands but also the ❸ inexpensive outfit like Gap and H&M.

I feel like I was sitting on the first row ❷ at a fashion show.

艾凡：我感覺就像坐在第一排的位置看時裝秀一樣。
凱莉：是啊！而且這裡不光只有昂貴的品牌，你也能找到像Gap、H&M等平價服飾店。

Okay! First thing first ❹, you like strapless, right? How's that one?

Are you kidding me? That brand costs an arm and a leg ❺! I can't afford it.

艾凡：好！先辦正事！你喜歡無肩帶的，對吧？那件怎麼樣？
凱莉：喔，別鬧了！那個牌子超貴的，我付不起。

單字說明 ❶ 尋找 ❷ 排 ❸ 平價的 / 不昂貴的 ❹ 重要的事先做 / 先辦正事 ❺ 非常昂貴

Compared to Taiwan, the price is a bit lower.

Not to mention the sample sale; they make the price even more affordable.

SAMPLE SALE

艾凡：不過，比起來，還真的比台灣的精品便宜一些。
凱莉：更不用提那些樣品特賣會了，價錢又更划算。

Oh my god! It's the NBA Store!❶ Can I go? I won't take too long. In and out, just a quickie.❷

艾凡：那裡有NBA 專賣店耶！我可以進去看看嗎？我不會花太多時間，進去一下下就
出來，很快！

Did you see the crowd over there?❸

Oh, that's the famous Saint Patrick ❹Cathedral. It's the most beautiful cathedral I have ever seen.

艾凡：你有看到那邊聚集的人潮嗎？

凱莉：喔！那間是聖派翠克天主教堂，非常有名！是我看過最漂亮的教堂。

購物、參與節慶活動&觀賞比賽的美式口語

Chapter 2

 單字說明　❶ NBA專賣店　❷ 匆忙之下完成的事　❸ 聚集的人潮　❹ 大教堂　　**085**

1 Since you are here, you can't miss that spot.

Great! I need to sit down, anyway. My feet are killing me.

凱莉：既然都來了，你就不能錯過那個景點。
艾凡：太好了，我需要順便休息一下，我的腿好痠痛。

I need a massage as a **2** reward for being your shopping partner.

Never gonna happen! (LOL)

艾凡：我需要一套按摩當作今天陪逛的酬勞。
凱莉：不可能。（大笑）

But I do know a best hot dog **3** stand nearby. Are you hungry yet?

Starving! What makes the hot dog stand so special?

The owner **4** is from Germany. They only use the sausages **5** from their country. You have to try then you will get it.

凱莉：但我知道附近有一間最棒的熱狗攤。你餓了沒？

艾凡：餓死了！為什麼那間熱狗攤這麼特別？

凱莉：他們的老闆來自德國，只用德國進口的香腸。你一定要試一試才會知道！

單字說明 **1** 既然 **2** 回饋／酬勞 **3** 攤子 **4** 老闆／擁有者 **5** 臘腸／香腸

一定要知道的**單字及用語**！

跟著Kari和Ivan逛完第五大道後，
別忘了繼續學習其它與本單元相關的道地美語常用單字及用語！

jewelry [ˋdʒuəlrɪ] 珠寶
I bought a piece of jewelry for my birthday.
我買了一件珠寶送給自己當生日禮物。

pearl
[pɝl]
珍珠

diamond
[ˋdaɪəmənd]
鑽石

crystal
[ˋkrɪstl̩]
水晶

necklace
[ˋnɛklɪs]
項鍊

ring
[rɪŋ]
戒指

jade
[dʒed]
玉

bracelet
[ˋbreslɪt]
手環

high heels 高跟鞋
This new pair of high heels hurt my feet.
這雙新的高跟鞋弄痛我的腳。

小補帖 **last season** 過季的
I don't care if this is from last season.
我不在乎這件衣服是不是過季的。

material [məˋtɪrɪəl] 材質
Can you tell me what the material of that bag is?
你可以告訴我那個包包的材質是什麼嗎？

display [dɪˋsple] 展示品

You can buy this with 50% off; it is a display item.

這件是展示品,你可以用五折的價錢買回去。

tag [tæg] 標籤

I want to know the price, but I can't find the tag.

我想知道價錢,但我找不到標籤。

Good!

cutting [ˋkʌtɪŋ] 剪裁

Do you see the cutting? This is a very fine work.

你有看到剪裁嗎?這是一件很精細的作品。

fit [fɪt] 合適

The dress fits you well. You look good in this.

這件洋裝很適合你,你穿起來很好看。

earthy [ˋɝθɪ] 大地色系的

As for the colors, I prefer earthy.

至於顏色呢,我喜歡大地色系。

How to wash? 怎麼清洗

How do you wash this jacket?
你怎麼洗這件外套？

dry clean 乾洗

hand wash 手洗

decline [dɪ`klaɪn] 拒絕

I am sorry, sir! But your card has been declined!
先生，很抱歉！你的卡無法使用。

credit card 信用卡

Do you accept credit card?
你們接受信用卡消費嗎？

price difference 價差

There is a huge price difference of these two shirts.
這兩件襯衫價差很大。

tight budget 預算很緊 / 預算有限

I can't afford that watch. I have a tight budget.
我買不起那隻錶，我的預算有限。

小補帖 **LOL (laugh out loud)** 大聲笑

註 為網路語言，為減少打字字數而簡化而成的用語，其他類似例子：NP (No problem) / BRB (be right back) / TYL (talk to you later)

購物、參與節慶活動&觀賞比賽的美式口語　Chapter **2**

來做練習吧！Let's practice

學習完本單元的單字及用語後，趕緊來做些練習，加深印象。

1 I am _____ _____ _____ a dress for a friend's wedding!

我要找一件可以穿去朋友婚禮的洋裝！

2 That brand costs an _____ and a _____ ! I can't afford it.

那個牌子超貴的，我付不起。

3 I am sorry, sir! But your card has been _____ !

先生，很抱歉！你的卡無法使用。

4 I do know a best hot dog _____ nearby.

我知道附近有一間最棒的熱狗攤。

5 You can buy this with 50% off; it is a _____ item.

這件是展示品，你可以用五折的價錢買回去。

6 This new pair of _____ _____ hurt my feet.

這雙新的高跟鞋弄痛我的腳。

7 I need a massage as a _____ for being your shopping partner.

我需要一套按摩當作今天陪逛的酬勞。

8 I don't care if this is from _____ _____ .

我不在乎這件衣服是不是過季的。

9 There is a huge _____ _____ of these two shirts.

這兩件襯衫價差很大。

10 _____ you are here, you can't miss that spot.

既然都來了，你就不能錯過那個景點。

解答

1. in search of 2. arm / leg 3. declined 4. stand
5. display 6. high heels 7. reward 8. last season
9. price difference 10. Since

參與熱鬧的節慶活動

Day 10 學習量：單字70個 / 會話用語40則

來洛克斐勒中心（Rockefeller Center）參加聖誕樹點燈儀式

人稱紐約市裡的綠洲，在繁忙的第五大道上，一個即使被購物商場和商業大樓包圍卻充滿綠意的休憩角落！絕不可錯過的是聖誕節的聖誕樹點燈儀式，今天就跟著凱莉和艾凡一起，享受紐約早到的聖誕氣氛。

MP3 10

The annual Christmas tree lighting is today! Why don't we join the crowd?

I've marked the Rockefeller Christmas tree lighting a "must" before I even landed.❶

凱莉：今天聖誕樹點燈耶，我們去湊湊熱鬧吧。

艾凡：早在我到達之前，就把洛克斐勒聖誕樹點燈儀式列為一項我必做的事了。

Ouch! That lady just stepped on my toe!

It's a ❷ zoo in here! Stay with me! Don't get lost!

艾凡：哎唷！那個小姐踩到我了。

凱莉：這裡擠得亂七八糟，你要跟好，不要走丟了！

That scene looks familiar. I am sure I've seen it somewhere.

On TV, every morning! The leader of NBC news is filmed right here.

艾凡：這個景象好熟悉，我確定在什麼地方看過。

凱莉：在電視上，每天早上！NBC新聞的片頭就是在這拍的。

  ❶ 降落 ❷ 動物園／人擠人的地方／亂糟糟的地方

艾凡：你看，下面有人在溜冰耶。
凱莉：對啊！那裡叫做下層廣場，每年的十月到隔年四月都開放成溜冰場。

凱莉：你有看到那兩棟大樓中間的那些噴泉嗎？那叫做「海峽花園」。

艾凡：另一邊那棟最高的就是GE大樓了。
凱莉：順便告訴你，NBC新聞的總部，就在GE大樓裡。如果你想的話，你還可以參加「NBC導覽團」，在那你會學到有關NBC的一切。

Chapter 2 購物、參與節慶活動＆觀賞比賽的美式口語

單字說明　❶ 溜冰　❷ 總部

I'll think about it! Hey, I can see the stage clearly❶ from here!

Let's just settle here and appreciate the show. Oh, no!

❷Now what?

艾凡：我會好好考慮的。從這裡可以
　　　很清楚地看到舞台耶。

凱莉：那我們就坐這吧，好好的欣賞表演！哎唷！
艾凡：又怎麼啦？

I just spilled❸ my coke. Clumsy me!

It's okay! I got it.

凱莉：我剛剛打翻了我的可樂！我真是個冒失鬼！
艾凡：沒關係！我來處理就好！

註：
海峽花園一邊的大廈是屬於法國的產業
──法國大廈；而另一邊的高樓卻是英國
人的財產──大英帝國大廈，這就像是把
英國法國隔開的英吉利海峽，因而得名
「海峽花園」。

　單字說明　❶ 清楚的　❷ 又怎麼了？　❸ 打翻 / 濺出

off

一定要知道的單字及用語！

跟著Kari和Ivan逛完洛克斐勒中心後，
別忘了繼續學習其它與本單元相關的道地美語常用單字及用語！

off

off

broadcast [`brɔdˌkæst] 廣播 / 廣播節目
The interview will be broadcast next Monday.
這段訪談將於下週一播出。

trailer [`trelə] 預告片
After seeing the trailer, I decide to go to see that movie.
看過預告之後，我就決定去看那部電影了。
subtitle [`sʌbˌtaɪtl] 字幕
caption [`kæpʃən] 字幕

clumsy [`klʌmzɪ] 冒失的
She is a clumsy girl. She always breaks things.
她是一個冒失的女孩，總是打破東西。

step on me 踩到我了
Watch out! You step on me!
請你小心點！你踩到我了！

somewhere [`sʌmˌhwɛr] 某處
I can't find my watch, but I am sure it is somewhere in my room.
我找不到我的錶，但我確定一定在我房間的某個角落。

mark [mark] 標記
He has a birth mark on his back.
他背上有一個胎記。

購物、參與節慶活動&觀賞比賽的美式口語

Chapter 2

off

anchor [ˋæŋkə] 主播

He is the anchor of the morning news.
他是晨間新聞的主播。

cameraman [ˋkæmərəˌmæn] 攝影師

John is a cameraman; he works for Discovery.
約翰是一名攝影師，他在探索頻道工作。

leader [ˋlidə] 片頭

The leader of the local news channel is funny.
那個地方新聞頻道的片頭很好笑。

channel [ˋtʃænl] 頻道

Can you switch to channel 65?
你可以把頻道轉到六十五台嗎？

小補帖 **channel** [ˋtʃænl] 海峽

The English Channel separates France from England.
英吉利海峽隔開法國和英國。

小補帖 **host** [host] 主持人

Opera is one of the most popular hosts in the states.
歐普拉是美國最受歡迎的主持人之一。

skyrocket [`skaɪˌrakɪt]
摩天大廈

You can see numbers of skyrockets in Manhattan.
在曼哈頓你可以看到很多的摩天大樓。

headquarters
[`hɛd`kwɔrtɚz] 總部
The headquarters of our company is located in Paris.
我們公司的總部在巴黎。

rink [rɪŋk] 溜冰場
Rockefeller Center rink is a world-known rink.
洛克斐勒廣場的溜冰場舉世聞名。

branch
[bræntʃ]
分公司 / 分部

I got it 我來就好

A: Let me help you!
B: Thank you, but it's okay! I got it.
A：我幫你吧！
B：謝謝你！不過沒關係，我來就好。

settle [`sɛtl̩] 坐下 / 安頓

Why don't you settle the children in the hotel first? That is much safer.
你怎麼不把小孩先安頓在飯店？這樣安全多了。

settle down 安頓下來
settle for 勉強接受

Chapter 2
購物、參與節慶活動&觀賞比賽的美式口語

❶ You can see numbers of _____ in Manhattan.

在曼哈頓你可以看到很多的摩天大樓。

❷ He is the _____ of the morning news.

他是晨間新聞的主播。

❸ It's a _____ in here! Stay with me! Don't get lost!

這裡擠得亂七八糟，你要跟好，不要走丟了！

❹ I just _____ my coke.

我剛剛打翻了我的可樂！

❺ Hey, I can see the stage _____ from here!

從這裡可以很清楚地看到舞台耶。

❻ Can you switch to _____ 65?

你可以把頻道轉到六十五台嗎？

❼ I can't find my watch, but I am sure it is _____ in my room.

我找不到我的錶，但我確定一定在我房間的某個角落。

❽ I've marked the Rockefeller Christmas tree lighting a " must " before I even

_____ .

早在我到達之前，就把洛克斐勒聖誕樹點燈儀式列為一項我必做的事了。

❾ The _____ of our company is located in Paris.

我們公司的總部在巴黎。

❿ She is a _____ girl. She always breaks things.

她是一個冒失的女孩，總是打破東西。

解答

1. skyrockets 2. anchor 3. zoo 4. spilled 5. clearly
6. channel 7. somewhere 8. landed 9. headquarters
10. clumsy

現場看籃球比賽最熱血！

Day 11 學習量：單字100個 / 會話用語35則

去麥迪遜廣場花園（Madison Square Garden）幫尼克隊加油

紐約第七大道上有一個很特別的花園，叫做「麥迪遜廣場花園」。在這個花園裡，你看不到花與蝴蝶，卻看得到熱血奔騰的NBA球賽。凱莉和艾凡今天要到麥迪遜廣場花園替尼克隊加油，我們也一起去吶喊吧！

MP3 11

I'll meet you up at 7th ave entrance at 7 tonight!

Sure! Let's rock it tonight!

凱莉：七點在麥迪遜花園第七大道入口見喔！
艾凡：好的！今晚瘋狂一下吧。

Hey, what took you so long? The game has started!

MADISON SQUARE

❶ The traffic jam! Sorry to keep you waiting.

凱莉：你怎麼這麼久？比賽已經開始了。
艾凡：塞車！不好意思喔，讓你等這麼久。

DE-FENSE!
DE-FENSE!

It is the Knicks' ball now!

❷ Blocking foul No.3 Shawne Williams.

Great! Now they get to go to the free-throw line.

（群眾鼓譟）防守！防守！
艾凡：現在是尼克隊進攻。

廣播：三號尚恩威廉斯！阻擋犯規！
艾凡：這下好了吧！現在對方可以站上罰球線了。

單字說明 ❶ 塞車／交通堵塞 ❷ 阻擋犯規

艾凡：只剩一分鐘就中場休息了。
凱莉：你有看到嗎？這個裁判在搞什麼！

凱莉：時間到！我們去買些熱狗和啤酒吧。
艾凡：好主意，我今天都還沒吃東西！

服務生：先生，我可以看你的身份証件嗎？
艾凡：不好意思，我沒帶！但我已經二十二
　　　歲了。

艾凡：真掃興！（真倒楣！）
凱莉：沒關係，我們可以一起喝。

Chapter 2
購物、參與節慶活動＆觀賞比賽的美式口語

單字說明　❶ ref(referee) 裁判　❷ 倒楣的事／麻煩　❸ 分享

101

Post, post! I can't believe he missed the shot!

Oh, no! We are down by 3.

艾凡：快快快！姿勢擺出來啊！我不敢相信他這球沒進！

凱莉：噢……天哪！現在已經落後三分了。

Look, we are on the screen! Smile! And wave.

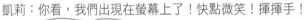
Knicks called 20 seconds time-out.

廣播：尼克隊叫出暫停。

凱莉：你看，我們出現在螢幕上了！快點微笑！揮揮手！

Oh my god! Three pointer for Bill Walker. That's a tough shot.

Hands down! We win by 1.

凱莉：我的天哪！比爾沃克投進了三分球！真是驚險的一球。

艾凡：比賽結束了，我們險勝一分。

單字說明 ❶ 螢幕

一定要知道的**單字**及**用語**！

跟著Kari和Ivan逛完麥迪遜廣場花園後，
別忘了繼續學習其它與本單元相關的道地美語常用單字及用語！

小補帖 **field goal** 投球命中

小補帖 **field goal percentage** 投球命中率

小補帖 **scoring** [ˋskorɪŋ] 得分

three-point shot / three pointer 三分球

free throw 罰球

draft [dræft] 選秀

小補帖 **buzzer** [ˋbʌzɚ]（比賽用的）蜂鳴器

power forward 大前鋒

shooting guard 得分後衛

point guard 控球後衛

forward (F) [ˋfɔrwɚd] 前鋒

小補帖 **guard (G)** [gɑrd] 後衛

small forward 小前鋒

center (C) [ˋsɛntɚ] 中鋒

foul [faul] 犯規
elbowing [ˈɛlboɪŋ] 打拐子
blocking foul 阻擋犯規

小補帖 fast break 快攻
小補帖 assist [əˈsɪst] 助攻
小補帖 double dribble 兩次運球

dribble [ˈdrɪbl] 運球

steal [stil] 抄截

flagrant foul 惡性犯規

ejection [ɪˈdʒɛkʃən] 驅逐出場

disqualification
[dɪsˌkwɑləfəˈkeʃən]
犯滿離場（又稱「畢業」）

double-team 雙人包夾

block shot 阻攻 / 蓋火鍋

小補帖 **defensive basket interference**
防守方干擾投籃得分

小補帖 **delay of game**
阻礙比賽之正常進行

rebound [rɪˋbaʊnd] 籃板球
bank shot 擦板球
bank [bæŋk] 籃板
brick [brɪk] 碰到籃板或籃框但未進的球

小補帖 **defensive rebound**
防守籃板球

小補帖 **offensive rebound**
進攻籃板球

charging foul 帶球撞人

90 : 89

10 : 01

小補帖 **first half** 上半場

小補帖 **expiration** 比賽時間終了

小補帖 **first (second, third, fourth) period**
比賽的第一（第二、第三、第四）節

小補帖 **five ticks left on the (game clock / shot clock...)**
（全場比賽 / 時限鐘上的）時間剩下五秒鐘

購物、參與節慶活動&觀賞比賽的美式口語

Chapter 2

來做練習吧！ Let's practice

學習完本單元的單字及用語後，趕緊來做些練習，加深印象。

1 Look, we are on the _____ !

你看，我們出現在螢幕上了！

2 The _____ _____ ! Sorry to keep you waiting.

塞車！不好意思喔，讓你等這麼久。

3 Did you see that? The _____ is messing things up.

你有看到嗎？這個裁判在搞什麼！

4 _____ _____ ! We win by 1.

比賽結束了，我們險勝一分。

5 It's okay! You can _____ mine!

沒關係，我們可以一起喝。

6 _____ _____ ! Let's get some hot dog and beer!

時間到！我們去買些熱狗和啤酒吧。

7 Sorry, I don't _____ _____ _____ me!

不好意思，我沒帶！

8 There is only one minute to _____ _____ .

只剩一分鐘就中場休息了。

9 _____ _____ to me! I haven't eaten today.

好主意，我今天都還沒吃東西！

10 _____ _____

阻擋犯規

解答

1. screen 2. traffic jam 3. ref / referee 4. Hands down
5. share 6. Time's up 7. have it with 8. half time
9. Sounds good 10. blocking foul

搭乘交通工具

一起去探索中央車站（Grand Central Terminal）的十一個祕密

凱莉和朋友約在位在中央車站大名鼎鼎的生蠔餐廳吃飯，順便帶著艾凡參觀了這座全世界最大，甚至最美的車站……

MP3 12

Do you know what the **①largest** **②train station** in the world is?

Who doesn't? It's Grand Central Terminal.

凱莉：你知道全世界最大的車站是哪一個嗎？ 艾凡：當然知道啊！不就是中央車站嗎？

Haha, you are right! I have a dinner date at the Oyster Bar restaurant in Grand Central. Why don't you come with me?

My pleasure.**③**

凱莉：哈哈！你答對了！我今天跟朋友約在中央車站裡的生蠔餐廳吃飯，一起去吧！
艾凡：那是我的榮幸！

This restaurant must have a long history.

You can say that again! Don't underestimate **④** it, pal! It is highly recommended by many food critics.

艾凡：這個餐廳看起來還真有歷史。
凱莉：是啊！朋友，你可別小看它喔，很多美食評論家都給予高度評價。

單字說明 ❶ 大的 ❷ 火車站 ❸ 樂意 / 榮幸 ❹ 低估

艾凡：有什麼值得一試嗎？

凱莉：這裡的生蠔一定得吃吃看！再來你一定要試試他們的蛤蠣濃湯。

艾凡：你有聽説過中央車站的祕密嗎？

凱莉：喔！你説那十一個祕密啊？你知道幾個？

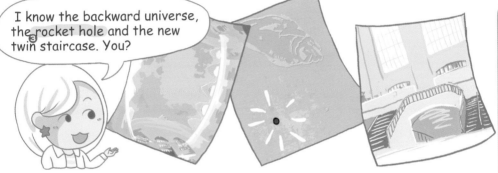

凱莉：我只知道相反的天花板、天花板上的洞，和不對稱的樓梯，你呢？

艾凡：我知道永遠不正確的時刻表、迴音廊，和羅斯福總統的祕密通道！我就只知道這些了。

單字說明　❶ 生蠔／牡蠣　❷ 特色／招牌菜　❸ 中央車站天花板上的洞是當年送火箭到中央車站展覽時，不小心戳壞天花板所留下的，因此被稱為火箭洞（rocket hole）。　❹ 中央車站裡有個迴音廊，只要對著牆壁輕輕地說話，站在另一邊的人就能清楚地聽見你所説的。（whisper 輕聲說話）

① I feel like I've taken a time machine back to the old days every time I stepped in here.

凱莉：當我踏進這裡，就像是搭了時光機回到以前。

True! We have Mrs. Jackie Kennedy to thank for that. She ② fought hard to keeping this precious building.

艾凡：是啊！多虧賈桂林夫人保住了這珍貴的建築。

So, where are we going to next?

Chrysler Building is ③ around the corner. Let's take a look.

艾凡：我們接下來要去哪呢？
凱莉：克萊斯勒大廈就在附近，去看看吧！

Nice taste! Chrysler Building is also ④ a masterpiece of Installment in many architects' eyes. ⑤

I have been thinking about going there! That's my favorite building on earth.

艾凡：我一直很想去看看！那是我最喜歡的建築物！
凱莉：好眼光，這同時也是許多當代建築師眼中裝置藝術建築學的傑作！走吧。

單字說明 ① 時光機 ② 對抗／爭執 ③ 在附近 ④ 傑作 ⑤ 裝置藝術

一定要知道的**單字及用語**！

跟著Kari和Ivan逛完中央車站後，
別忘了繼續學習其它與本單元相關的道地美語常用單字及用語！

step [stɛp] 踏進
I scared him when I stepped in his room quietly.
我輕輕地走進他房間，結果嚇到他了。

lean against 靠著
You are not supposed to lean against the door! It's very dangerous.
你不應該緊靠車門，這樣很危險！

platform [`plæt͵fɔrm] 月台
I saw her off at the platform.
我在月台上幫她送行。

platform gap 月台間隙

train number XXXX XXXX號列車
Attention please, train number 123 is arriving on the south bound track.
請注意，123號南下列車即將進站。

小補帖 **terminal** [`tɝmənl] 航廈 / 轉運站 / 大車站
Your boarding gate is at terminal 7.
您的登機門在第七航廈。

小補帖 **port** [port] 港口 / 港灣
小補帖 **pier** [pɪr] 碼頭
小補帖 **airport** [`ɛr͵port] 機場

111

car [kar] 車子 / 車廂

Your seat is on car 5, seat 17.
你的座位在第五車第十七號。

catch the train 趕火車

Would you please hurry?
I have a train to catch.
你可以快一點嗎？我要趕火車。

backwards [ˋbækwədz] 反方向地

Do you know how to drive backwards?
你知道怎麼倒著開車嗎？

around the corner
就在附近了 / 也差不多了

（corner 角落 / 轉角）

Jerry is right around the corner;
he will be here shortly.
傑瑞就在附近了，他馬上就到。

小補帖 **backward** [ˋbækwəd] 委婉的

"Shoot" is a backward way to say "shit."
Shoot是shit的委婉說法。

architect [ˈɑrkəˌtɛkt] 建築師
He is the architect of this building.
他是這棟大樓的建築師。

lawyer [ˈlɔjəʳ] 律師

doctor [ˈdɑktəʳ] 醫師
surgeon [ˈsɝdʒən]
外科醫師

food critic 食物評論家
（critic 評論家）
He is working hard to be a food critic.
他很努力想要成為一位食評家。

accountant
[əˈkauntənt]
會計師

have someone to thank for
該感謝……
For this beautiful garden, I have my garden planner to thank for.
我要謝謝我的園藝設計師給我這麼漂亮的花園。

pleasure [ˈplɛʒəʳ] 榮幸
A: Thank you for coming with me!
B: The pleasure is all mine.
A: 謝謝你陪我來。
B: 別客氣，是我的榮幸。

Chapter **2**
購物、參與節慶活動&觀賞比賽的美式口語

小補帖 **mean** [min] 意指
I didn't mean to hurt anyone.
我沒有想要傷害任何人。

小補帖 **history** [ˈhɪstərɪ] 歷史 / 曾發生過的事或紀錄
According to his history, I don't believe him.
從他的紀錄來看，我不相信他。

來做練習吧！ Let's practice

學習完本單元的單字及用語後，趕緊來做些練習，加深印象。

① The oysters are their _____ .

這裡的生蠔是招牌菜。

② I feel like I've taken a _____ _____ back to the old days every time I stepped in here.

當我踏進這裡，就像是搭了時光機回到以前。

③ He is the _____ of this building.

他是這棟大樓的建築師。

④ Jerry is right _____ _____ _____ ; he will be here shortly.

傑瑞就在附近了，他馬上就到。

⑤ Have you _____ _____ the secrets of Grand Central?

你有聽說過中央車站的祕密嗎？

⑥ Do you know what the largest _____ _____ in the world is?

你知道全世界最大的車站是哪一個嗎？

⑦ You are not supposed to _____ _____ the door! It's very dangerous.

你不應該緊靠車門，這樣很危險！

⑧ I have a dinner date at the Oyster Bar restaurant in Grand Central. Why don't you _____ _____ me?

我今天跟朋友約在中央車站裡的生蠔餐廳吃飯，一起去吧！

⑨ He is working hard to be a _____ _____ .

他很努力想要成為一位食評家。

⑩ I saw her off at the _____ .

我在月台上幫她送行。

解答

1. specialty 2. time machine 3. architect
4. around the corner 5. heard of 6. train station
7. lean against 8. come with
9. food critic 10. platform

約會要遲到了！

約好到百老匯劇場（Broadway Shows）看歌劇，要來不及了！

來到紐約絕不可錯過的重頭戲，就是百老匯劇場。這裡充滿了融合歌劇（Operetta）、雜耍綜藝歌舞秀（Vaudeville）、富麗秀（Follies）以及音樂歌舞輕喜劇（Musical Comedy）的精彩表演。

星期三中午，凱莉提早下課，打算帶艾凡一起去看場百老匯表演，約好了在售票亭見面，艾凡卻遲遲還沒出現……

MP3 **13**

凱莉：嗨，艾凡！我今天放假，你想不想去看百老匯？
艾凡：當然想啊，太好了！那我們要在哪邊碰面？

（凱莉正在留言給艾凡）喂，你到了嗎？我已經等了十五分鐘了！艾凡，我們快要趕不上了，聽到留言回電給我！

艾凡：真的很對不起！我在看職棒世界大賽，看著就忘了時間！
凱莉：你什麼？！你知道我們錯過了整場秀嗎？而且，我還花了一百二十塊買票!

單字說明　❶ would you like to 意思和 do you want to...一樣，但是比較禮貌，較建議使用　❷ 碰面　❸ 語音留言（紐約的地鐵沒有收訊，所以紐約人很習慣留言，等到對方下車就可以聽得到。）　❹ 聽到這個（留言）之後回電給我（常用口語）　❺ 錯過　❻ 而且 / 不僅如此

艾凡：嗯！我的錯！那些票可以退嗎？讓我補償你！喝杯咖啡怎麼樣？我不是故意的，而且我都道歉了！你到底要我怎麼樣？

凱莉：道歉沒有用！算了，我要回家了！

艾凡連續道歉了好多天，最後凱莉終於原諒他。

艾凡：請問我有這個榮幸邀請你和我一起去看百老匯嗎？
凱莉：（大笑）除非你停止這些虛偽的舉止，然後讓我選要看哪一部。

單字說明　❶ 不是故意的　❷ 榮耀／榮幸　　117

購物、參與節慶活動&觀賞比賽的美式口語　Chapter 2

I thought you would never ask! Such a relief.

❶ Do you like musical comedies? Do you have anything in mind?

艾凡：我還怕你不問呢！我真是鬆了一口氣。

凱莉：你喜歡音樂喜劇嗎？你有沒有什麼意見？

Since this is my first Broadway show, can we go with something more classic? ❷

Not a problem. In that case, *Phantom of the Opera* would be my first choice.

(asking bashfully) And one more thing; is there any way we can get the less expensive tickets?

Of course, you stingy! We can ❸ get up to 50% off tickets online! Let me show you!

BUY TICKET 50% off

艾凡：既然這是我的第一部百老匯劇，我們可以選擇比較經典的嗎？

凱莉：當然沒問題！這樣的話，那《歌劇魅影》就是我的第一選擇。

艾凡：（靦腆地問）還有一件事，我們有可能拿到便宜一點的票嗎？

凱莉：當然可以啊，你這個小氣鬼！我們可以在網路上拿到最高五折的票，來，我教你怎麼買！

註：百老匯四大名劇分別為安德魯洛依韋伯的《貓》、《歌劇魅影》與鮑勃力和勳博格的《悲慘世界》、《西貢小姐》，這四部劇被列為音樂劇歷史上的四大名劇。

單字說明 ❶ 喜劇 ❷ 經典的 ❸ 五折（依此類推七折是30% off；九折是10% off）

一定要知道的**單字**及**用語**！

跟著Kari和Ivan逛完百老匯後，
別忘了繼續學習其它與本單元相關的道地美語常用單字及用語！

stingy [ˈstɪndʒɪ] 小氣的 / 小氣鬼
Saving money doesn't mean you should be stingy.
要存錢不代表你要很小氣。

only if 除非
Only if you buy me the dinner,
or I am gonna tell on you.
除非你請我吃晚餐，不然我就告你的密。

Chapter **2**
購物、參與節慶活動&觀賞比賽的美式口語

phony [ˈfonɪ] 虛偽的 / 假的
She is a phony girl.
她是一個虛偽的女孩。

gesture [ˈdʒɛstʃɚ] 姿態 / 姿勢
He crossed his arms in a gesture of defending.
他雙手交叉以示防衛。

mean [min]（做形容詞）
形容某人很惡劣、卑鄙
You are so mean.
你好惡劣。
She looks like a mean girl.
她看起來不是個好女孩。

my bad 我的錯（口語說法）

It's my bad; I didn't think it through.
是我的錯，我沒有想清楚。

make it up (to / for someone)
補償某人

Let me make it up to you. I should have believed you!
我該相信你的，讓我補償你。

forget it 算了 / 不管了

Forget it! I am not angry anymore!
算了，我已經不氣了。

off the hook 放過 / 原諒

Please let Christy off the hook.
She has determined to amend.
原諒克莉絲蒂吧，她已經決定改過自新了。

such a relief 真是鬆了一口氣

When I knew I passed the test, that's such a relief.
當我知道我通過測驗時，我真是鬆了一口氣。

lose track of time 錯過時間 / 沒有注意時間

He was doing his research and lost track of time.
他在做研究，忙得忘記時間了。

returnable [rɪˋtɝnəbl̩]
可退換的

I am buying this shirt for my friend,
but I am not sure about her size.
Is this returnable?
這衣服是幫我朋友買的，但我不確定她的尺寸！
請問這可以退換嗎？

bashful [ˋbæʃfəl] 靦腆的

She is too bashful to talk to the singer.
她太害羞了，所以不敢去跟那位歌手說話。

continue [kənˋtɪnju] 繼續 / 延續

He continued his speech after drinking water.
他喝過水後繼續演講。

have anything in mind
有意見嗎？有想法嗎？

What should we eat for lunch?
Do you have anything in mind?
我們中餐要吃什麼？你有想法嗎？

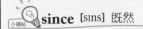 **since** [sɪns] 既然

Since you don't care at all, I'll just leave.
既然你一點都不在乎，那我就離開。

 since [sɪns] 自從

I have lived here since I was 6
我從六歲就住在這。

購物、參與節慶活動&觀賞比賽的美式口語

Chapter 2

來做練習吧！Let's practice

學習完本單元的單字及用語後，趕緊來做些練習，加深印象。

❶ I didn't _____ _____ and I said sorry!

我不是故意的，而且我都道歉了！

❷ _____ _____ _____ that, I spent $120 for the tickets.

而且，我還花了一百二十塊買票！

❸ Saving money doesn't mean you should be _____ .

要存錢不代表你要很小氣。

❹ What should we eat for lunch? Do you have anything _____ _____ ?

我們中餐要吃什麼？你有想法嗎？

❺ It's _____ _____ ; I didn't think it through.

是我的錯，我沒有想清楚。

❻ Where should we _____ _____ ?

那我們要在哪邊碰面？

❼ Please let Christy _____ _____ _____ . She has determined to amend.

原諒克莉絲蒂吧，她已經決定改過自新了。

❽ _____ _____ ! I am not angry anymore!

算了，我已經不氣了。

❾ Do I have the _____ of inviting you to a Broadway show with me?

請問我有這個榮幸邀請你和我一起去看百老匯嗎？

❿ I am buying this shirt for my friend, but I am not sure about her size. Is this _____ ?

這衣服是幫我朋友買的，但我不確定她的尺寸！請問這可以退換嗎？

解答

1. mean it 2. On top of 3. stingy 4. in mind 5. my bad
6. meet up 7. off the hook 8. Forget it 9. honor
10. returnable

在戶外利用wi-fi上網

在書香環繞的布萊恩公園（Bryant Park）和紐約市立圖書館（NY Public Library） 享受無線上網

還記得電影《明天過後》裡的避難所嗎？記得慾望城市凱莉夢想中的婚禮殿堂嗎？這全美最大的市立圖書館，已有一百零七年的歷史，緊鄰在旁的布萊恩公園也不遑多讓，堪稱是紐約市活動最多的公園，夏天的紐約，別忘了時不時踏進美麗的布萊恩公園，絕對會有驚喜的！

MP3 14

凱莉：你準備好了嗎？我們該出門囉。
艾凡：好！我不知道百老匯也在公園演出耶。

凱莉：這是布萊恩公園最膾炙人口的活動之一，每年都會邀請百老匯的明星到公園裡獻唱最受歡迎的歌曲。

凱莉：而且看到百老匯明星們不是穿著戲服的樣子也滿有趣的。
艾凡：好像是你意外看到他們在後台排練一樣。

  ❶ 表演 ❷ 最受歡迎的 / 最熱門的 ❸ 戲服 / 為表演而穿的服裝

❶ Besides, HBO cooperates with Time Warner Cable in presenting the classics on the big screen every summer. This free, ten-week outdoor film series provides the ultimate setting for film lovers in New York City.

凱莉：除此之外，每年夏天，HBO和華納公司會合作挑選幾部經典的電影，在公園裡播放。這免費的、連續十周的戶外電影活動，提供愛電影的紐約人一個最好的去處。

Do you see the ❷ carrousel over there! That's a signature of Bryant Park, too.

I notice that there are many people using laptops here! Don't tell me there's wi-fi access!

Bingo! You're welcome to move your office here!

凱莉：你看那邊！你有看到旋轉木馬嗎？
這也是布萊恩公園的標誌喔！

艾凡：我發現好多人在這裡用手提電腦！這裡該不會有無線網路吧？
凱莉：恭喜答對！歡迎你把這當作你的辦公室！

❸ What's the building behind?

艾凡：後面那棟建築是什麼？

單字說明　❶ 合作　❷ 旋轉木馬　❸ 在後面的

購物、參與節慶活動&觀賞比賽的美式口語　Chapter 2

That's New York Public Library. Have you seen *The Day After Tomorrow* or *Sex and the City*? Do you have any recollection❶ of that?

凱莉：喔！那是紐約市立圖書館，你看過《明天過後》和《慾望城市》嗎？有沒有想起什麼？

Oh, yes! The ❷ shelter and the wedding!

You bet! Let's sit down! The show is about to start!

艾凡：我想起來了！是電影裡的避難所和凱莉的婚禮。
凱莉：答對了！先坐下吧！表演差不多要開始了！

單字說明 ❶ 回憶 / 記憶 ❷ 避難所

一定要知道的**單字及用語**！

跟著Kari和Ivan逛完布萊恩公園後，
別忘了繼續學習其它與本單元相關的道地美語常用單字及用語！

symbol [ˋsɪmb!] 象徵
Doves are a symbol of peace.
鴿子是和平的象徵。

backstage
[ˋbækˋstedʒ] 後台
I am so curious about the fashion show backstage.
我對時裝秀的後台很好奇。

ultimate [ˋʌltəmɪt] 最終的
He worked so hard and won the ultimate honor.
他努力獲得最後的榮耀。

rehearsal [rɪˋhɝs!] 排練 / 預演
They are in rehearsal for the show tonight.
他們為了今晚的表演正在彩排。

buff [bʌf] 迷 / 愛好者（口語）
I am a movie buff.
我是個電影迷。

provide [prə`vaɪd] 提供
Free buffet is provided in the lobby.
大廳備有免費自助餐。

library [`laɪˌbrɛrɪ] 圖書館
I borrowed several books form the library.
我從圖書館借了幾本書。

setting [`sɛtɪŋ] 佈景 / 環境
This is a perfect setting for wedding.
這是個辦婚禮的完美環境。

parasol [`pærəˌsɔl] 陽傘
We stand a parasol for some shadow.
我們立了一支陽傘遮陽。

lawn [lɔn] 草地
No dogs are allowed in the lawn.
這片草地禁止帶狗。

bench [bɛntʃ] 長凳 / 板凳
The little girl and her mother are both sitting on the bench reading.
那個小女孩和媽媽一起坐在板凳上看書。

series [ˋsirɪz] 連續 / 系列

A series of bummers ruined my vacation.
一連串的倒楣事毀了我的假期。

accidently [ˏæksəˋdɛntlɪ] 意外地

I accidently broke my mom's vase.
我不小心打破了我媽的花瓶。

notebook [ˋnotˏbʊk]
/ **laptop** [ˋlæptɑp] 筆記型電腦

I always bring my laptop
when I travel.
我旅行時總會帶著我的筆電。

desktop [ˋdɛsktɑp]
桌上型電腦

wireless

[ˋwaɪrlɪs] 無線的
The wireless keyboards
are very convenient.
無線鍵盤很方便。

shelter [ˋʃɛltɚ] 避難所

Movie theaters are my shelters from
my endless work.
電影院是我逃離無止盡工作的避難所。

refugee [ˏrɛfjuˋdʒi] 難民

The refugee need water, food and
clothes.
難民們需要水，食物和衣物。

來做練習吧！ Let's practice

學習完本單元的單字及用語後，趕緊來做些練習，加深印象。

❶ Do you have any _____ of that?

有沒有想起什麼?

❷ It's also interesting to see the Broadway show stars out of their _____ .

而且看到百老匯明星們不是穿著戲服的樣子也滿有趣的。

❸ The _____ need water, food and clothes.

難民們需要水，食物和衣物。

❹ The _____ keyboards are very convenient.

無線鍵盤很方便。

❺ I am so curious about the fashion show _____ .

我對時裝秀的後台很好奇。

❻ They invite Broadway shows stars to the park to perform their biggest _____ .

布萊恩公園每年都會邀請百老匯的明星到公園裡獻唱最受歡迎的歌曲。

❼ What's the building _____ ?

後面那棟建築是什麼?

❽ Besides, HBO _____ with Time Warner Cable in presenting the classics on the big screen every summer.

除此之外，每年夏天，HBO和華納公司會合作挑選幾部經典的電影，在公園裡播放。

❾ I _____ broke my mom's vase.

我不小心打破了我媽的花瓶。

❿ A _____ of bummers ruined my vacation.

一連串的倒楣事毀了我的假期。

解答

1. recollection 2. costumes 3. refugee 4. wireless
5. backstage 6. hits 7. behind 8. cooperates
9. accidently 10. series

登高看夜景

Day 15 學習量：單字65個 / 日常用語40則

登上帝國大廈（Empire State Building），站在紐約頭上看夜景

凱莉的爸媽上禮拜來紐約玩，因為時間緊湊來不及去帝國大廈，於是留了兩張票，讓兩個年輕人享受浪漫的夜景！

MP3 15

凱莉：嘿！你記得上個禮拜我爸媽來紐約玩？

艾凡：記得啊！他們人都很好。

凱莉：你知道嗎？他們留了兩張票給我。
　　　我們今晚去帝國大廈吧。

艾凡：一張票要十八塊耶，那我要
　　　付你錢。

凱莉：不用了！他們的行程太緊湊了所以沒空去，如果你不去，那票也是浪費掉啊！

艾凡：那謝謝囉！我請你吃晚餐代替。

單字說明　❶ 親切的／友善的　❷ 你知道嗎？（不是真的問句，是一種吸引對方注意或興趣的方式。）
　　　　　❸ 很緊湊的行程　❹ 作為替代

They make it a very **strict** security check here ❶

Yes, they ❷ tend to be more careful after 911.

艾凡：這裡的安檢還真嚴格。

凱莉：對啊，九一一事件之後，安檢都更小心了。

Chapter **2** 購物、參與節慶活動&觀賞比賽的美式口語

Look! They take photos for every visitor. You can decide ❺ if you want to buy the pictures afterwards.

凱莉：你看！他們幫每個來參觀的旅客照相，他們可以看過照片再決定要不要買。

How ❸ tall is this building?

It is a 102-**story** ❹ building, 1,250 ft (381 meters) tall.

❻ (flash) I was not ready yet!

艾凡：這棟建築物有多高？

凱莉：全部是一百零二樓，一千兩百五十英呎（三百八十一公尺）高。

艾凡：（閃光燈）我還沒準備好耶……

 單字說明 ❶ 非常嚴格的、周詳的 ❷ 有……的傾向 ❸ 建築物、人、物的高度 **133**
❹ 層／樓 ❺ 在此作為「是否」 ❻ 閃光燈

This view is phenomenal.①

I am in love with what I see.②

凱莉：這個夜景簡直是不可思議。
艾凡：我已經愛上我所看到的一切了。

Now we know why King Kong had to climb on here.③

凱莉：現在我們知道為什麼金剛非得爬上
　　　這裡了。

Besides that, I also realize why they had Meg Ryan and Tom Hanks meet up here.

艾凡：除此之外，我也了解為什麼他們要讓
　　　梅格萊恩和湯姆漢克斯在這裡相遇了。
　　　（為電影《西雅圖夜未眠》的場景）

It is getting chilly and windy up here.④

I'll just grab some souvenirs and we'll head back.⑤

凱莉：天氣開始變冷，風也變大了。
艾凡：我到樓下買個紀念品我們就回家吧。

単字説明　❶ 驚人的／不可思議的　❷ 和……沉溺在愛河中　❸ 爬／攀　❹ get + adj. 變得……
❺ 紀念／紀念品

134

一定要知道的**單字**及**用語**！

跟著Kari和Ivan逛完帝國大廈後，
別忘了繼續學習其它與本單元相關的道地美語常用單字及用語！

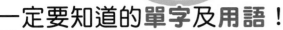

observatory [əbˋzɝvə͵torɪ]
瞭望台 / 觀測台

The observatory is located on the 86th floor.
觀景台位在八十六樓。

86 F

floor [flor] 樓層

I live on the 5th floor.
我住在第五樓。

chilly [ˋtʃɪlɪ]
冷颼颼的 / 寒風刺骨的

It is chilly out there.
外面好冷喔。

windy [ˋwɪndɪ]
風勢強勁的

It is getting windy with the approaching hurricane.
隨著颶風的接近，風變大了。

5F

intersection [͵ɪntɚˋsɛkʃən]
交叉口 / 十字路口

My apartment is at the intersection of E7th street and 2nd ave.
我的公寓在東七街和第二大道交叉口。

flight [flaɪt] 樓梯的一段

His studio is two flights up.
再往上兩層就是他的工作室了。

flight [flaɪt] 航班 / 飛行

I overslept this morning and missed my flight.
我今天早上睡過頭所以錯過我的班機。

Chapter **2**

購物、參與節慶活動&觀賞比賽的美式口語

locker [ˋlakɚ] 置物櫃

There are lockers where you can put your
luggage in on the ground floor.
一樓有你可以放東西的置物櫃。

check [tʃɛk] 寄放 / 托運

Do you need to check your luggage?
你有行李需要托運嗎？

afterwards [ˋæftɚwɚdz] 事後 / 之後
I need to check the system afterwards.
我等等得去查看一下這個系統。

**leave something with someone /
leave someone something**
把……留下給某人

I left you some books on the night stand.
我在邊桌上留了一些書給你。

security check 安全檢查

You have to go through the security check to get into
ESB (Empire State Building.)
你必須要通過安檢才能進入帝國大廈。

waste [west] 浪費

Going to that restaurant is a waste of time and money.
去那間餐廳吃飯簡直是浪費錢又浪費時間。

buy someone dinner
幫……買晚餐（有請客的意思）

Let me buy you dinner for your help.
讓我請你吃晚餐以謝謝你的幫忙。

besides [bɪ`saɪdz] 除此之外
（除了本身之外，其他也是）

Besides me, Helen is also from California.
除了我之外，海倫也從加州來。

except [ɪk`sɛpt] 除此
（除了本身之外，其他都不）

I don't like any seafood except fish.
除了魚之外，其他所有的海鮮我都不喜歡。

have to 當時非得……

I had to make that decision;
he didn't leave me any choices.
我當時非得這麼做，他並沒有給我任何選擇。

cost [kɔst] 價值（多少錢）

This dress costs me 125 dollars.
這件洋裝花了我一百二十五塊。

購物、參與節慶活動&觀賞比賽的美式口語

Chapter **2**

來做練習吧！ Let's practice

學習完本單元的單字及用語後，趕緊來做些練習，加深印象。

❶ _____ _____ _____ ? They left me two tickets.

你知道嗎？他們留了兩張票給我。

❷ I _____ _____ make that decision; he didn't leave me any choices.

我當時非得這麼做，他並沒有給我任何選擇。

❸ My apartment is at the _____ of E7th street and 2nd ave.

我的公寓在東七街和第二大道交叉口。

❹ I'll just grab some _____ and we'll head back.

我到樓下買個紀念品我們就回家吧。

❺ Yes, they _____ _____ be more careful after 911.

對啊，九一一事件之後，安檢都更小心了。

❻ It is _____ _____ with the approaching hurricane.

隨著颶風的接近，風變大了。

❼ Their schedule was _____ _____ _____ go there.

他們的行程太緊湊了所以沒空去。

❽ Let me _____ _____ _____ for your help.

讓我請你吃晚餐以謝謝你的幫忙。

❾ You have to go through the _____ _____ to get into Empire State Building.

你必須要通過安檢才能進入帝國大廈。

❿ I need to check the system _____ .

我等等得去查看一下這個系統。

解答

1. You know what 2. had to 3. intersection
4. souvenirs 5. tend to 6. getting windy 7. too tight to
8. buy you dinner 9. security check 10. afterwards

Chapter 3

點餐用餐、餐廳候位 &問路的美式口語

在下城區（Downtown）的八個景點學習點餐、用餐、餐廳候位及問路的相關用語

採買日常用品

Day 16 學習量：單字95個 / 日常用語35則

到最時尚的雀兒喜市場（Chelsea Market）採買食材及生活必需品

星期六早晨，天氣很晴朗。凱莉打算帶艾凡去逛逛她最喜歡的市場，買些新鮮的食材。坐落在第九大道和十六街交叉口，雀兒喜市場是一棟紅磚建築。在這裡，你幾乎可以找到所有你想要的東西：設計師款服飾、高檔精緻的食物、新鮮的水果、蔬菜、海鮮、餐廳、甜點、廚房用品、甚至是書。快進來吧，這裡有很多驚喜等著你！

MP3 16

凱莉：（正在梳她的頭髮）今天天氣很好耶，你有沒有什麼計畫？

艾凡：（正在做早餐）沒有什麼特別的計畫耶，你咧？

凱莉：我在想，可能去買些日用品。我們的衛生紙快沒了。

艾凡：嗯！這樣的話，那我應該要跟你一起去！我相信，我可以幫上你的忙。

  ❶ 刷牙／梳頭（梳頭也可用comb） ❷ make breakfast 做早餐（做飯的動詞用make）
❸ 指的是採購日用品或是買菜 ❹ 在那個情況下／那樣的話

That's very nice of you! I'll be ready in 15 minutes! ❶ BTW, the bacon smells good!

Thank you. I'll save you some! Take your ❷ time. Let me know when you are all set.

凱莉：你真好！那給我十五分鐘準備。喔，對了，培根聞起來好香喔！

艾凡：謝謝！我會幫你留一點！你慢慢來，準備好了再跟我說！

Here is Chelsea Market, one of my favorite markets of all time. Have you ever been here?

凱莉：這裡就是雀兒喜市場，我最喜歡的市場之一。你有來過嗎？

Never! This place is amazing; they sell everything here. Look! We can see that bakery baking bread behind the glass wall.

BREAD

Welcom

艾凡：從來沒有耶！這個地方好棒，什麼都有賣！你看，那個玻璃牆後面，那間麵包店正在烤麵包。

單字說明　❶ BTW（by the way）順帶一提，相當於口語中的「喔，對了」 ❷ 慢慢來

Okay! I am going to get some lobsters for dinner. I'll be at the seafood booth in the corner if you need me!

No problem! I'll pick up some cheese at that gourmet deli.❶

凱莉：我要去買一些龍蝦當晚餐，你要找我的話，我會在角落的那個海鮮攤。

艾凡：沒問題！那我去那個高級美食舖買一些起司。

Oh, they have the best goat-cheese in town! And don't forget to go to Anthropology; it's worth a visit. See you at the front door at 3.

凱莉：喔，他們的羊奶起司很棒喔！不要忘了去「Anthropology」，那裡很值得逛一逛。
　　　三點大門口囉！

Thank you, Kari! I will grab toilet paper on the way out! Later!

艾凡：好啊！謝謝你，凱莉！我出來的時候會順便買衛生紙的！拜拜！

單字說明 ❶ 高級美食

一定要知道的**單字及用語**！

跟著Kari和Ivan逛完雀兒喜市場後，
別忘了繼續學習其它與本單元相關的道地美語常用單字及用語！

building [ˋbɪldɪŋ] 建築物

I live in that gray building.
我住在那棟灰色的建築物裡。

branch [bræntʃ] 分店

Starbucks has a large number of branches around the world.
星巴克在全世界有非常多的分店。

pay phone 公共電話

Is there any pay phone nearby? I left my cell phone at home.
這附近有公共電話嗎？我把手機忘在家裡了。

crosswalk [ˋkrɔsˌwɔk] 行人穿越道

It is safer walking on the crosswalk.
走在行人穿越道上比較安全。

sign [saɪn] / **road sign** 標誌 / 路標

The sign says "detour." We should make a u-turn here.
那個標誌寫「繞道」，我們應該要在這裡迴轉。

avenue [ˋævəˌnju] 大道

Chelsea market is on the 9th avenue.
雀兒喜市場在第九大道。

block [blɑk] 街口

The restaurant is only a block away.
那間餐廳就在下一條街上。

Chapter 3
點餐用餐、餐廳候位&問路的美式口語

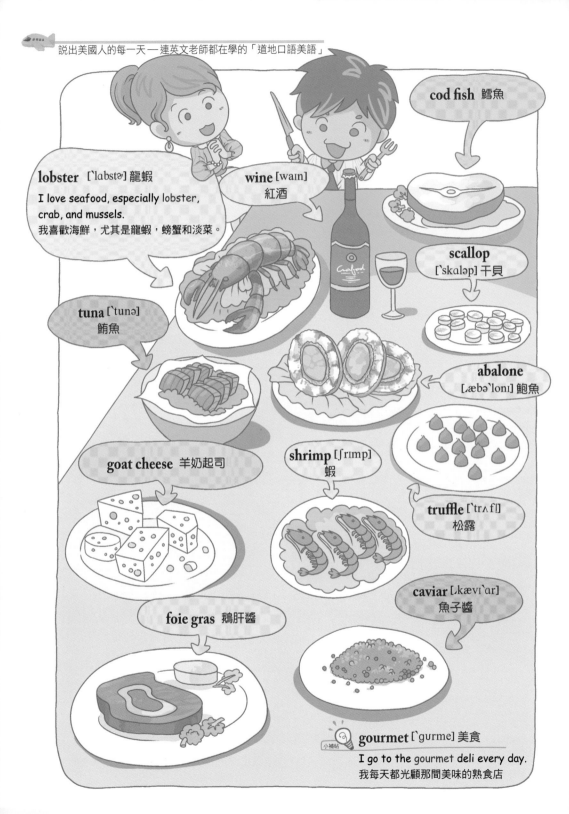

cod fish 鱈魚

lobster [`labstɚ] 龍蝦
I love seafood, especially lobster, crab, and mussels.
我喜歡海鮮，尤其是龍蝦，螃蟹和淡菜。

wine [waɪn] 紅酒

scallop [`skɑləp] 干貝

tuna [`tunə] 鮪魚

abalone [͵æbə`lonɪ] 鮑魚

goat cheese 羊奶起司

shrimp [ʃrɪmp] 蝦

truffle [`trʌf!] 松露

foie gras 鵝肝醬

caviar [͵kævɪ`ɑr] 魚子醬

小補帖 gourmet [`gurme] 美食
I go to the gourmet deli every day.
我每天都光顧那間美味的熟食店

lingerie [ˋlænʒəˏri]
女性內衣睡衣 / 女性貼身衣物

He bought his girlfriend some lingerie for her birthday.
他買了一些貼身衣物給女友當生日禮物。

小補帖 **pajamas** [pəˋdʒæməs]
睡衣（口語常簡稱PJ）

I just got up and was still in my pajamas.
我才剛起床，還穿著睡衣。

well-known [ˋwɛlˋnon] 有名的
Miss Amerson is a well-known tailor.
愛默生小姐是一個很有名的裁縫師。

apron [ˋeprən] 圍裙
I always wear apron when I cook.
我做菜的時候一定會穿上圍裙。

outfit [ˋautˏfɪt] 裝備 / 整套的服裝
That tie and shirt makes a nice outfit.
那領帶和襯衫這樣配成一套很好看。

Chapter **3**
點餐用餐、餐廳候位&問路的美式口語

① Well, _____ _____ _____ , I should go with you. I

believe you can use my help.

嗯！這樣的話，那我應該要跟你一起去！我相信，我可以幫上你的忙。

② I always wear _____ when I cook.

我做菜的時候一定會穿上圍裙。

③ It is safer walking on the _____ .

走在人行道上比較安全。

④ _____ _____ _____ . Let me know when you are all set.

你慢慢來，準備好了再跟我說！

⑤ Starbucks has a large number of _____ around the world.

星巴克在全世界有非常多的分店。

⑥ Miss Amerson is a _____ tailor.

愛默生小姐是一個很有名的裁縫師。

⑦ The restaurant is only a _____ away.

那間餐廳就在下一條街上。

⑧ I am thinking about _____ _____ .

我在想，可能去買些日用品。

⑨ I just got up and was still in my _____ .

我才剛起床，還穿著睡衣。

⑩ We are _____ _____ _____ toilet paper.

我們的衛生紙快沒了。

解答

1. in that case 2. apron 3. crosswalk
4. Take your time 5. branches 6. well-known 7. block
8. grocery shopping 9. pajamas 10. running out of

到肉品包裝區（Meatpacking District）享受滿足味蕾的法式早午餐
期中考結束的那個週末，兩人為了慶祝，來到肉品包裝區的Pastis吃早午餐，順便逛逛近幾年翻身崛起的新興時尚中心──肉品包裝區。

MP3 **17**

艾凡：我的天啊！這間餐廳已經擠翻了。我們有訂位嗎？
凱莉：帕蒂斯是一間非常有名的餐廳，要兩個禮拜前訂位才有位子。

服務生：嗨，早安！需要先來些飲料嗎？

艾凡：水就可以了。
凱莉：我要蘋果汁，謝謝。

服務生：你們的飲料到了！請問現在可以幫您點餐了嗎？還是您需要多點時間呢？

 ❶ 非常擁擠的狀況　❷ 預訂／預約　❸ 非常受歡迎的（人／事／地）　❹ 之前／先前　❺ 飲料
❻ （當副詞）首先　❼ I'd like = I would like，意思等同於I want，但是比較有禮貌，建議使用！
❽ take someone's order　幫某人點餐

Sorry, I am still deciding. Okay, a BLT sandwich for me! Thank you.

Oh, yes, please! I'd like an Egg Benedict for me and a garden omelet for share.

凱莉：喔，好啊，麻煩你！我自己要一個班　艾凡：不好意思喔，我還沒決定！好吧，
　　　尼迪克蛋，然後一個田園蛋捲一起吃。　　　　那我要一個生菜培根三明治。

(40 minutes later)

Can I take the empty plate for you? Does everything taste okay for you?

服務生：我可以幫您把空盤收起來嗎？請問餐點都合您胃口嗎？

I think we have to walk to work off the large meal.

I see many galleries and designer brands.

凱莉：我想我們得散個步來消耗剛剛那頓大餐了！
艾凡：我看到很多藝廊和設計師品牌。

單字說明　❶ 決定　❷ 空的　❸ 盤子　❹ 必須要　❺ 散步　❻ 設計師品牌

Chapter 3　點餐用餐、餐廳候位&問路的美式口語

This is a **❶new-raising** neighborhood, very **❷trendy** and **stylish.❸**

Kari, do you know what that amazing building is?

凱莉：這是一個新崛起的區域，非常的時髦有型。
艾凡：凱莉，你知道那棟漂亮的建築物是什麼嗎？

That's the Standard Hotel. It **is rated❹** the most unusual and significant NY building in years by NY Observers. High Line Park is another **❺spot** that you don't want to miss!

凱莉：那是史丹達大飯店，被紐約觀察家時報評選為近年來最特別、最有意義的建築。
高線公園則是另一個你不會想錯過的景點。

This park was **❻rebuilt** from an **❼obsolete freight❽** train track. **❾Artworks** are presented with a **❿rotating** schedule in and around the High Line.

凱莉：這個公園是從廢棄的貨運鐵道重建起來的。各項藝術作品也輪流在高線公園裡及
四周展出。

單字說明 ❶ 新興的／新崛起的 ❷ 時髦的 ❸ 有型的／流行的 ❹ 被評選為／被評定為 ❺ 景點／地點
❻ 重建／改建 ❼ 廢棄的／淘汰的 ❽ 貨運 ❾ 藝術作品 ❿ 輪流

一定要知道的**單字及用語**！

跟著Kari和Ivan逛完肉品包裝區後，
別忘了繼續學習其它與本單元相關的道地美語常用單字及用語！

look forward to + Ving / N.
對……非常期待
I am so looking forward to it.
我很期待。

I am looking forward to seeing you.
我很期待見到你。

be rated 被評選為 / 被評定為
This movie is rated R.
這部電影被訂為限制級。
（R：restricted 限制級）

make reservations 預約 / 訂位
Where did you make reservations for the dinner?
你晚餐在哪裡訂位？

unusual [ʌnˋjuʒʊəl] 不平常的 / 特別的
It is unusual for him coming home so late.
他很少這麼晚回家。

小補帖 **in advance** 事前
We should call him in advance.
我們事先應該打電話給他。

Chapter **3**
點餐用餐、餐廳候位&問路的美式口語

153

recommendation
[ˌrɛkəmɛnˋdeʃən]

推薦的（餐點、物品……）

Do you have any recommendations?
你有任何推薦的嗎？

Egg Benedict 班尼狄克蛋

將半熟的水煮荷包蛋及火腿一起放在英式鬆餅上的一道料理，吃的時候搭著流下的蛋汁，非常美味。

omelet [ˋɑmlɪt]
煎蛋包／蛋捲

將料包在香嫩的煎蛋裡，是早午餐很受歡迎的菜色。

sunny-side up
荷包蛋（單面煎）

over easy
荷包蛋（兩面微煎）

scrambled eggs
炒蛋

boiled eggs
水煮蛋

significant [sɪgˋnɪfəkənt]
有意義的／意味深長的

This is a significant book.
這是一本很有意義的書。

for share 分享（餐點）

We order a 12oz stake for share.
我們點了十二盎司的牛排一起分享。

free refill 免費續杯

Do you have free refill on coke?
你們可樂有免費續杯嗎？

sparkle ['spɑrkl] 閃耀 / 發泡

sparkling water 氣泡水

註 在美國因為氣泡水很盛行，而且自來水是可以直接飲用的，所以當你要說要water時，服務生會接著問"Tap water or sparkling?"（一般水還是氣泡水？）。有時候會多問bottled water（瓶裝水），指的是一些比較高級的礦泉水。以上除了tap water之外，其他的都要收費喔！

BLT

註 bacon（培根）、lettuce（萵苣）、tomato（蕃茄）三種的組合。因為風行多年，遂成經典，簡稱為BLT。

Tap Wa

wrap up 打包帶走

Please wrap the chicken wings up!
請把雞翅打包！

Chapter 3 點餐用餐、餐廳候位&問路的美式口語

1 Please _____ the chicken wings _____ !

請把雞翅打包！

2 This is a _____ book.

這是一本很有意義的書。

3 May I _____ your _____ now or do you need more time?

請問現在可以幫您點餐了嗎？還是您需要多點時間呢？

4 Do we have a _____ ?

我們有訂位嗎？

5 It _____ _____ the most unusual and significant NY building in

years by NY Observers.

它被紐約觀察家時報評選為近年來最特別、最有意義的建築。

6 Do you have _____ _____ on coke?

你們可樂有免費續杯嗎？

7 We order a 12oz stake _____ _____ .

我們點了十二盎司的牛排一起分享。

8 I am _____ _____ _____ seeing you.

我很期待見到你。

9 This park was _____ from an obsolete freight train track.

這個公園是從廢棄的貨運鐵道重建起來的。

10 I see many galleries and _____ _____ .

我看到很多藝廊和設計師品牌。

解答

1. wrap / up 2. significant 3. take / order
4. reservation 5. is rated 6. free refill 7. for share
8. looking forward to 9. rebuilt 10. designer brands

來焙烘坊選購甜點

來格林威治村（Greenwich Village）買知名排隊甜點，
順便體驗嬉皮、爵士等不同文化

今天是凱莉的生日，艾凡記得凱莉說過她很喜歡一家在格林威治村的甜點，所
以他決定去尋找，給她一個驚喜。

MP3 **18**

凱莉：早安！你趕著出門嗎？
艾凡：對啊，我跟朋友約了十五分鐘後碰面。

艾凡：格林威治村真漂亮，這裡有好多賣
　　　精品的小商店。

艾凡：我知道紐約最有名的披薩店之一，
　　　約翰披薩就在這裡。

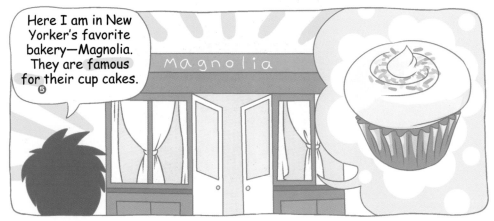

艾凡：我到了！紐約客最愛的烘培屋——木蘭花烘焙。他們的杯子蛋糕非常有名。

❶ 匆忙／催促　❷ in＋時間長度，表示多久之後，如：in 2 hours, in 5 weeks...　❸ 精品／女裝
❹ 專賣披薩的餐廳　❺ 因……而出名

❶ Yet Kari is a big fan of their Banana pudding and ❷ red velvet cake. I take one each of them for Kari.

艾凡：但凱莉卻對他們的香蕉布丁和紅絲絨蛋糕很著迷。我各拿了一個給凱莉。

There is a huge ❸ line out of a shop. I am curious.❹

艾凡：我看到一家店前面大排長龍！我很
好奇。

It is Marc by Marc Jacobs, a retail factory shop of Marc Jacobs.❺

艾凡：原來是「Marc by Marc Jacobs」，一間
零售知名品牌馬克賈伯商品的小店！

點餐用餐、餐廳候位&問路的美式口語

Chapter 3

The ❻ stuff there is creative, colorful and much less expensive.

艾凡：裡面賣的東西都很有創意，色彩豐富而且非常便宜。

單字說明　❶ 然而 / 但是（作連接詞）　❷ 紅絲絨蛋糕（一種顏色為鮮紅，有淡淡巧克力味，口感細膩柔軟如絲
絨的蛋糕。在國外很受歡迎！velvet：天鵝絨）　❸ 非常大的　❹ 好奇的　❺ 零售　❻ 東西 / 商品

> I see a lot of cool people and **hipsters** here. They look so upfront and happy. This area is also the center of the 50/60 pop music and Jazz.

艾凡：在這裡我看到很多很酷的人和嬉皮。他們看起來都很坦率而且很快樂。這裡也是五零到六零年代流行歌曲和爵士樂的中心。

> If you are a jazz lover, please do visit Blue Note and Village Vanguard.

艾凡：如果你是個爵士樂愛好者，請一定要到「Blue Note」和「Village Vanguard」這兩家店朝聖。

> (Ivan's cell phone is ringing. It's a text message from Kari)
>
> Hey, we are in Fat Cat, the bar next to the subway exit. Meet us here. Fat Cat is a **local hangout** where you can enjoy nightly live music. They also have pool, ping pong, foosball and many other **entertainment choices.**

（艾凡的電話響了，原來是凱莉傳來的簡訊）

嘿！我們在肥貓酒吧，就是靠近地鐵出口的那間酒吧，來這找我們吧！肥貓酒吧是個當地人常常去，每晚都有現場音樂表演的好去處。他們也提供撞球、桌球、手足球和很多其他的娛樂。

 ❶ 嬉皮 ❷ 流行音樂 ❸ 爵士樂 ❹ 當地的 ❺ 常去的地方 / 舒服的地方
❻ 娛樂的 / 娛樂性質的 ❼ 選擇

一定要知道的**單字及用語**！

跟著Kari和Ivan逛完格林威治村後，
別忘了繼續學習其它與本單元相關的道地美語常用單字及用語！

yet [jɛt] 還沒（作副詞）

I am not home yet.
我還沒到家。

center [ˋsɛntɚ] 中心

She stood in the center of the crowd and gave a speech.
她站在人群中央，開始演講。

factory [ˋfæktərɪ] 工廠

His father works in a factory.
他的父親在工廠工作。

by + 時間點　在……之前

I should be home by 5 p.m.
我下午五點以前會到家。

less [lɛs]　較少的 / 較差的

My watch is less expensive than yours.
我的手錶比你的便宜。（less expensive 比較便宜，因為cheap另有低級之意，所以比較價錢時，建議使用less expensive，而非cheaper。）

shop [ʃɑp] 商店

There are a lot of gift shops around Time Square.
時代廣場附近有很多紀念品專賣店。

bakery [ˈbekərɪ] 麵包店 / 烘焙坊

The bakery downstairs makes delicious cookies.
樓下麵包店做的餅乾很好吃。

bake [bek] 烘培 / 烤

pudding [ˈpʊdɪŋ] 布丁

Have you tried Sue's bread pudding? Yum!
你有吃過蘇做的麵包布丁嗎？很好吃！

each [itʃ] 每個 / 各個

Each girl here gets a gift.
在這裡的每個小女生都拿到禮物。

favorite [ˈfevərɪt] 特別喜歡的人或物

Ivan is my favorite student.
艾凡是我最疼愛的學生。

creative [krɪˋetɪv] 有創意的
This artist is very creative.
這個藝術家很有創意。

neon [ˋniˌɑn] 霓虹燈

SEXY

Let's party!

colorful [ˋkʌləfəl]
多采多姿的／顏色豐富的
I like the colorful decoration.
我喜歡這顏色豐富的裝飾。

hipster [ˋhɪpstə]
嬉皮／追趕時髦的人
註 嬉皮（hippie）一字原為hipster，是「超時髦的人」的意思，愛迷幻搖滾、民俗服飾、崇向自由性愛也接受東方宗教和哲學。

🍦 **pool** [pul] / **billiards** [ˋbɪljədz] 撞球
小補帖

🍦 **ping pong** 桌球／乒乓球
小補帖

🍦 **foosball** [ˋfuzˌbɔl] 手足球
小補帖

Chapter 3
點餐用餐、餐廳候位&問路的美式口語

來做練習吧！Let's practice

學習完本單元的單字及用語後，趕緊來做些練習，加深印象。

① The _____ downstairs makes delicious cookies.

樓下麵包店做的餅乾很好吃。

② My watch is _____ _____ than yours.

我的手錶比你的便宜。

③ They are _____ _____ their cup cakes.

他們的杯子蛋糕非常有名。

④ Fat Cat is a local _____ where you can enjoy nightly live music.

肥貓酒吧是個當地人常常去，每晚都有現場音樂表演的好去處。

⑤ There is a _____ _____ out of a shop.

我看到一家店前面大排長龍！

⑥ I like the _____ decoration.

我喜歡這顏色豐富的裝飾。

⑦ This area is also the center of the 50/60 _____ _____ and Jazz.

這裡也是五零到六零年代流行歌曲和爵士樂的中心。

⑧ This artist is very _____ .

這個藝術家很有創意。

⑨ Ivan is my _____ student.

艾凡是我最疼愛的學生。

⑩ The _____ there is creative and colorful.

裡面賣的東西都很有創意，色彩豐富。

解答

1. bakery 2. less expensive 3. famous for 4. hangout
5. huge line 6. colorful 7. pop music 8. creative
9. favorite 10. stuff

逛書店、有機食材市場和跳蚤市場

Day 19 學習量：單字75個 / 日常用語30則

前往聯合廣場（Union Square）逛最有名的二手書店、有機市場及跳蚤市場

週末，晴天，凱莉和艾凡要拆夥各自出外走走。艾凡打算去紐約最大的二手書店瞧瞧。凱莉也趕緊向他推薦其它幾個鄰近的必逛景點。

MP3 19

Hey, I am ❶heading out to meet my friends. Do you have any ❷plans today?

Yes, I am going to Strand Books.

凱莉：我要出門跟朋友碰面，你今天有要做什麼嗎？
艾凡：有啊，我今天要去河岸書店！

Yeah? Great! I go there a lot. Are you looking for anything ❸specific?

凱莉：真的嗎？真好！我常常去那裡，你有特別要找什麼嗎？

No, just looking around! My friend told me that's a huge ❹second-hand ❺bookstore.

艾凡：沒有耶，就隨便看看！我朋友説那是一間很大的二手書店。

  ❶ head out / to 出門 / 往……去 ❷ 計畫 ❸ 特定的 / 專門的 ❹ 二手的 ❺ 書店

凱莉：它真的是！很值得走一趟。那你知道怎麼去嗎？

艾凡：我知道！搭L車然後在第十四街下車。

凱莉：喔，你知道嗎？你應該也要去農貿市場，他們全都是來自附近的農場。

艾凡：嗯⋯⋯除非你要我幫你買東西！因為我沒有很熱衷於有機食品。

 單字說明　❶ 確實地 / 絕對地　❷ worth + Ving / N　值得⋯⋯　❸ 也　❹ 順道拜訪　❺ 崇拜者 / 喜愛者　❻ 有機的

There is also a flea① market for artists② and designers selling their own work too.

凱莉：那邊也有一個給藝術家或設計師賣自己作品的跳蚤市場。

That sounds③ much more tempting.

艾凡：聽起來有吸引力多了！

Okay, I should④ be home by 10 tonight. See you then.⑤

Sure! Have a nice day. ⑥Later!

凱莉：我應該晚上十點以前會到家，到時見囉。
艾凡：沒問題，祝你有美好的一天。拜拜！

STRAND Bookstore

168　單字說明　❶ 跳蚤市場 ❷ 賣 ❸ 聽起來 ❹ 應該 ❺ 那時 / 到時
　　　　　　 ❻ 等一下 / 晚點（有「晚點見」的意思，所以也當再見使用）

一定要知道的單字及用語！

跟著Kari和Ivan逛完聯合廣場後，
別忘了繼續學習其它與本單元相關的道地美語常用單字及用語！

green market
綠色市場 / 有機市場

📌 指的是販賣當地農場自產自銷商品的市場。通常都是有機作物。

local [ˋlok!] 當地的

Sue is a local. She grew up
in this neighborhood.
蘇是當地人，她在這一區長大。

veggie [ˋvɛdʒɪ] 素食者

He is a veggie; he only eats vegetable foods.
他是嚴格的素食主義者，只吃素食食品。

vegetarian [͵vɛdʒəˋtɛrɪən] 奶蛋素食者

**buy one
get
one free**
買一送一

only if 除非

Only if you want or I don't think
I can eat anymore.
除非你想要，不然我吃不下了。

organic [ɔrˋgænɪk] 有機的

They claim that everything they sell is organic.
他們宣稱賣的所有東西都是有機的。

take + 交通工具　搭／搭乘

I take subway to school every day.
我每天都搭地鐵上學。

Have a nice day!

🈲 是美國人說再見時常常附加的祝福語，對朋友或陌生人都可以用。有些時候，碰面的時候已經下午了，也可以俏皮的改成Have a nice rest of the day.（rest of the day：這天剩下的時間。）

get off　下車

Excuse me, I am getting off.
不好意思，我要下車。

get in / get on
上車

hop in / on
跳上（車、船）來吧

（俏皮的口語說法）

hang out 和朋友相聚／打發時間

I hung out with Jerry last night.
我昨天跟傑瑞出去。

hangout （做名詞用）

常常去的地方／可以舒服窩著的地方

bookstore [`buk͵stor] 書店
Strand Books is my favorite bookstore.
河岸書店是我最喜歡的書店。

stationery store
文具店

小補帖 **own** [on] 自己的 / 特有的
Johnny Depp has his own style.
強尼戴普有他自己獨特的風格。

designer [dɪ`zaɪnə] 設計師
Tom ford is a famous fashion designer.
湯姆福特是一個知名時裝設計師。

小補帖 **for your own good**
為了你自己好
註 通常在規勸時使用

tempting [`tɛmptɪŋ] 誘惑的 / 吸引人的
A trip to Las Vegas sounds tempting.
到拉斯維加斯旅遊聽起來很棒！

Welcome to Las Vegas

artist [`artɪst] 藝術家
Amy is a graffiti artist.
艾咪是一個塗鴉藝術家。

Chapter **3**
點餐用餐、餐廳候位&問路的美式口語

1 Tom ford is a famous fashion _____ .

湯姆福特是一個知名時裝設計師。

2 Hey, I am _____ _____ _____ meet my friends.

我要出門跟朋友碰面。

3 They claim that everything they sell is _____ .

他們宣稱賣的所有東西都是有機的。

4 You should also _____ _____ the Farmer's Market.

你應該也要去農貿市場。

5 I _____ _____ with Jerry last night.

我昨天跟傑瑞出去。

6 A trip to Las Vegas sounds _____ .

到拉斯維加斯旅遊聽起來很棒！

7 There is also a _____ _____ for artists and designers selling their own work too.

那邊也有一個給藝術家或設計師賣自己作品的跳蚤市場。

8 Are you looking for anything _____ ?

你有特別要找什麼嗎？

9 _____ _____ you want or I don't think I can eat anymore.

除非你想要，不然我吃不下了。

10 He is a _____ ; he only eats vegetable foods.

他是嚴格的素食主義者，只吃素食食品。

解答

1. designer 2. heading out to 3. organic 4. stop by
5. hung out 6. tempting 7. flea market 8. specific
9. Only if 10. veggie

糟糕！迷路了

在蘇活區（SOHO）迷了路，向路人問路……

艾凡拿著地圖，一個人坐地鐵到紐約最不可錯過的景點──蘇活區(SOHO: SOuth of HOuston Street)，除了打算大肆採購之外，還要去吃凱莉口中紐約最棒的早午餐。

MP3 20

(trying to figure out the direction with his map)

（看著地圖試著找出方向）

Excuse me, sir! Is Spring Street that way?

Yes, go straight and you will hit② Spring Street at the second traffic light. Are you looking for③ some place?

艾凡：不好意思，先生！史普林街是在那個方向嗎？
男子：是的，你直走，第二個紅綠燈就是史普林街。你在找什麼地方嗎？

Yes, you don't happen to④ know where Balthazar is, do you?

Oh, that! It is right at the⑤ corner of Spring and Crosby Street. No worries, you can't miss it.⑥

艾凡：對啊，你該不會剛好知道Balthazar餐廳在哪裡，對吧？
男子：喔！那間啊！他就剛好在史普林街和克羅斯貝街的轉角。別擔心，你不會找不到的。

No wonder people⑦ are crazy about SOHO. This place is amazing. I can window-shop all the⑧ high-end brands.⑨

艾凡：難怪大家都為蘇活區瘋狂，我可以逛遍所有高級的品牌，雖然我沒有錢買。

 ❶ 理出頭緒 ❷ 本意為打或打擊，也可當作碰到 / 到達 ❸ 找尋 ❹ 該不會，恰巧 ❺ 角落 / 轉角
❻ 錯過 ❼ 難怪 ❽ 只逛而不買（商店展示商品的櫥窗叫做window，window-shop就是只在櫥窗逛逛
看看，不一定會購買）❾ 高級的 / 昂貴的

艾凡：這裡到處都有很棒的藝廊，不管是經典的藝術作品或是現代藝術都看得到。你看，穿貂皮大衣的那位女士看起來好像某個名人。

艾凡：我看了一些攤販賣的東西，都是手工製作的，但是有點貴。我試著殺價。

艾凡：那的石板路和舊建築簡直就是絕配。我看到有街頭藝人在唱歌，我聽到都入神了。

單字說明　❶ 很棒的　❷ 藝廊／藝術品展示區　❸ 現代的／近代的　❹ 貂皮　❺ 大衣　❻ 攤販
❼ 手工製作的　❽ bargain / haggle　殺價（當名詞則指很划算的交易。）　❾ 石板路
❿ 古老的／舊的　⓫ 街頭藝人　⓬ lose time + Ving　做某事做到出神

艾凡：突然，有個女生拍我肩膀。

女生：先生，你踩到我的腳了。

艾凡：我覺得好丟臉。她笑了，還叫我不要在意。

艾凡：回家的路上，我順道去Dean&Deluca超市買了一些起司。

單字說明　❶ 突然間　❷ 輕拍　❸ 踩到　❹ 感到不好意思、丟臉　❺ 不要在意、沒什麼（用來回應對方說對不起或謝謝的時候。）　❻ on the way... 在……路上 / 在……途中　❼ 順道停留

一定要知道的**單字及用語**！

跟著Kari和Ivan逛完蘇活區後，
別忘了繼續學習其它與本單元相關的道地美語常用單字及用語！

lose track of time 忘記時間

I was talking with an old friend and lost track of time.
我剛在跟一個老朋友聊天聊到忘記時間了。

brunch [brʌntʃ] 早午餐

美國人假日習慣晚起，把早餐breakfast和
午餐lunch合在一起吃，所以稱為早午餐
brunch，也是少數白天可以合理飲酒的場
合。一般餐廳只有假日供應早午餐，通常
供應至下午四點。

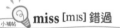**miss** [mɪs] 錯過

You can't miss it. It's a big building.
你不會錯過它的，那是很高的大樓。

no worries

不要擔心（意思等同於**don't worry**）

No worries, I'll be there on time!
不要擔心，我會準時到達！

high-end [haɪˋɛnd] 高價的／昂貴的

She is doing advertisement for high-end products.
她幫高級精品做廣告。

177

classic [`klæsɪk] 經典的 / 典型的

Phantom of the Opera is a classic Broadway show.
《歌劇魅影》是很經典的百老匯表演。

luxury [`lʌkʃərɪ] 奢侈的 / 奢華的

She leads a luxury life.
她過著很奢華的生活。

class [klæs] 氣質

Faith is a girl with real class.
費絲是一個很有氣質的女孩。

celebrity [sɪ`lɛbrətɪ] 名人 / 名流

There is a big chance to see celebrities in NYC.
在紐約市裡，很有機會看到名人。

elegant [`ɛləgənt] 高雅的

She looks elegant in that ivory dress.
她穿那件象牙白的洋裝看起來很高雅。

chic [`ʃik] 有品味的 / 時髦的

👉 chic中的ch 要發sh的音

collection [kəˈlɛkʃən] 收藏（品）

He has a great collection of Picasso's works.
他收藏有大量畢卡索的作品。

modern [ˈmɑdən] 現代的 / 摩登的

They went to an exhibition of modern art.
他們去了一個現代藝術的展覽。

discount [ˈdɪskaunt] 折扣

The boss gave me 20% off as a VIP discount.
老闆給我會員的八折折扣。

🔆 **a bargain**
小補帖　用很划算的價錢買到好東西

🔆 **You're getting it for a song!**
小補帖　這已經很便宜了！

🔆 **It's a steal!** 很划算的買賣
小補帖

🔆 **available** [əˈveləbl] 可用的 / 有空的
小補帖

Are you available tonight?
你今天晚上有空嗎？

來做練習吧！Let's practice

學習完本單元的單字及用語後，趕緊來做些練習，加深印象。

❶ She smiled and said " _____ _____ ."
她笑了，還叫我不要在意。

❷ Are you _____ tonight?
你今天晚上有空嗎？

❸ I check some street _____ out.
我看了一些攤販賣的東西。

❹ You don't _____ _____ know where Balthazar is, do you?
你該不會剛好知道Balthazar餐廳在哪裡，對吧？

❺ _____ _____ , I'll be there on time!
不要擔心，我會準時到達！

❻ There is a big chance to see _____ in NYC.
在紐約市裡，很有機會看到名人。

❼ Sir, you _____ _____ my feet.
先生，你踩到我的腳了。

❽ I was talking with an old friend and _____ _____ _____ time.
我剛在跟一個老朋友聊天聊到忘記時間了。

❾ _____ _____ people are crazy about SOHO.
難怪大家都為蘇活區瘋狂。

❿ The boss gave me 20% off as a VIP _____ .
老闆給我會員的八折折扣。

與服務生確認人數、排隊等候帶位

在東村（East Village）客滿的餐館與服務生確認人數、排隊等帶位

晚上十點，凱莉的同學打電話約凱莉一起去東村吃消夜。於是凱莉便邀請艾凡一起赴約。日本居酒屋、希臘烤肉餅、中式餃子、西班牙馬鈴薯蛋餅……通通都有。這裡是七零年代龐克文化的發源地，也是現在紐約的刺青重地。

MP3 **21**

凱莉：嘿，艾凡！你想去吃日式燒烤嗎？
艾凡：好啊！但現在嗎？我以為餐廳都已經關了。

凱莉：這裡的日本餐廳開到凌晨兩點左右。
艾凡：我不敢相信現在是晚上十一點半，看看這些人潮！每間店前面都有人排隊！

凱莉：他們說大概要等二十分鐘。
艾凡：不算太糟啊，我還以為會更久！

 ❶ be up for something 有興致做（某事） ❷ 我以為……（通常用在事實和自己認知不同的時候） ❸ 營業到……（有些店家不喜歡用close，所以問到幾點要說 How late do you stay open?） ❹ 擁擠的人群 ❺ 排隊的隊伍

凱莉：我們找個地方呼吸點新鮮空氣吧！我受不了這麼擠。

艾凡：喔，有人跟我說這附近有一家很有名的薯條店。

Chapter 3
點餐用餐、餐廳候位&問路的美式口語

凱莉：我知道啊！那間叫做波姆炸薯條。他們提供很多種類的沾醬。
艾凡：我們先吃點薯條墊墊肚子吧！

凱莉：好啊，我肚子餓得咕嚕咕嚕叫了。
艾凡：（邊說邊偷笑）那是你啊？我還以為是打雷了咧！

 ❶ 呼吸點新鮮空氣 ❷ 忍受 ❸ 被告知／聽說 ❹ 非常多種類的 ❺ 沾醬 ❻ 壓制／平息 **183**
❼ 飢餓 ❽ 胃 ❾ 發牢騷／咕噥聲 ❿ 偷笑／竊笑 ⓫ 雷聲

I am so **stuffed!** Can't even think about "food."

Me too! But what about Veniero? They make cheese cakes to **die for.**

凱莉：我吃得好撐！連想到「食物」這兩個字都很不舒服。

艾凡：我也是！不過，Veniero怎麼辦？他們的起司蛋糕好吃得不得了。

Next time you come here, **make sure** you walk around the whole neighborhood. Here is a lot more than just delicious food.

I'll **keep that in mind!** Thank you for **keeping me company** tonight.

凱莉：下次你來這裡，一定要記得好好逛逛這一區。這裡不只有好吃的食物，還有更多值得看的。

艾凡：我會記得的！謝謝你今晚陪我。

單字說明 ❶ 裝滿的 / 堆滿的（在這裡指把胃撐滿了。）❷ 死都願意（表示非常棒，例：food to die for就是美味到不行的食物 / job to die for 就是夢寐以求的工作。）❸ 確定 / 保證 ❹ keep... in mind 把……記在心上 / keep... company 和……做伴 / 陪在……旁邊

一定要知道的**單字**及**用語**！

跟著Kari和Ivan逛完東村後，
別忘了繼續學習其它與本單元相關的道地美語常用單字及用語！

Chapter **3**
點餐用餐、餐廳候位&問路的美式口語

wait for seating / wait to be seated
等候帶位
The lady wants us to wait here to be seated.
那位小姐要我在這裡等候帶位。

table for 2 兩人用餐
Hi, table for 2, please!
你好，請給我們兩個人的座位。

neighborhood [ˈnebɚˌhʊd] 區
（類似台北東區的概念，紐約很多區域都發展出自己的特色，每一區域neighborhood都有自己的名字，像是SOHO、 Chelsea……等）
Williamsburg is my favorite neighborhood in NYC.
威廉斯堡是我在紐約最喜歡的區。

in line 排隊
Sir, are you in line?
先生，你在排隊嗎？

cheese [tʃiz] 起司

Cheese cake is my all time favorite.
起司蛋糕是我永遠的最愛。

小補帖 **cheesy** [ˈtʃizɪ] 老套的 / 肉麻的

I don't really like that movie, too cheesy.
我不太喜歡那部電影，太肉麻了。

tipsy [ˈtɪpsɪ] 微醺的 / 喝醉的

Two cups of beer have made him tipsy.
兩杯啤酒下肚，他就有點醉了。

My stomach is grumbling.
我肚子餓到咕嚕咕嚕叫。

sake 清酒

Sake is a very famous Japanese liquor.
清酒是一種有名的日本酒。

put up with 忍受

Why do you put up with him? You don't have to!
你為什麼要忍受他?沒有必要啊!

💡 **company** [ˋkʌmpənɪ] 朋友 / 同伴
People are judged by the company they keep.
觀其友知其人。

already [ɔlˋrɛdɪ] 已經
You are late. He already left.
你遲到了,他已經先離開了。

💡 **keep** [kip] 維持

💡 **keep in touch** 保持聯絡

💡 **keep fit** 保持身材(苗條)

whole [hol] 整個 / 全部
The little girl ate the whole pie!
那個小女生把整個派都吃掉了!

來做練習吧！Let's practice

學習完本單元的單字及用語後，趕緊來做些練習，加深印象。

1 Are you _____ _____ a Japanese barbecue?

你想去吃日式燒烤嗎？

2 I am so _____ !

我吃得好撐。

3 I don't really like that movie, too _____ .

我不太喜歡那部電影，太肉麻了。

4 People are judged by the _____ they keep.

觀其友知其人。

5 They make cheese cakes to _____ _____ .

他們的起司蛋糕好吃得不得了。

6 Sure, my stomach is _____ .

好啊，我肚子餓得咕嚕咕嚕叫了。

7 Thank you for _____ me _____ tonight.

謝謝你今晚陪我。

8 Sir, are you _____ _____ ?

先生，你在排隊嗎？

9 Why do you _____ _____ _____ him? You don't have to!

你為什麼要忍受他？沒有必要啊！

10 The Japanese restaurants here _____ _____ till around 2 at night.

這裡的日本餐廳開到凌晨兩點左右。

解答

1. up for 2. stuffed 3. cheesy 4. company 5. die for
6. grumbling 7. keeping / company 8. in line
9. put up with 10. stay open

介紹一座城市

Day 22 學習量：單字55個 / 會話用語35則

生動地為朋友介紹下東城（Lower East Side）

凱莉和艾凡一起從威廉斯堡橋散步到下東城，計畫到Clinton St. Baking Co吃好吃又有名的鬆餅當早午餐，再好好一起逛逛這紐約最重要的次文化重地！

MP3 22

I didn't know Williamsburg and the Lower East Side ❶are connected. Many people are jogging ❷ or riding bicycles on ❸ the bridge.

艾凡：我不知道原來威廉斯堡和下東城有相連耶！好多人在橋上慢跑或騎腳踏車。

Look! Do you see the ❹graffiti over there? The colors are so bold! ❺

凱莉：你看！你有看到那裡的塗鴉嗎？用色好大膽！

I am ❻right above❼ Hudson river looking at the west ❽shore of Manhattan island. Too bad ❾ the ❿passing trains on the next track make a lot of noise.

I am so excited about going to the Haunted House! I go there every Halloween.

艾凡：我在哈德遜河的正上方遠眺曼哈頓島的西岸。可惜經過隔壁鐵道的列車太吵了。

凱莉：我好興奮喔，要去鬼屋了！我每年萬聖節都會去。

 單字說明　❶ be connected　有連結的　❷ 健走 / 慢跑　❸ 騎腳踏車　❹ 牆上塗鴉　❺ 大膽的 / 創新的　❻ 在此做加強語氣用　❼ 在上方　❽ 水岸　❾ 只可惜……　❿ 經過的

艾凡：抱歉！恐怕你得一個人去了！我一向不喜歡那些恐怖的東西。嘿！我們到了！

凱莉：喔，拜託！不要那麼掃興嘛！他們的鬆餅被評為紐約第一！我真希望我有吃完店
　　　裡所有東西的食量。

艾凡：這一區好特別！街道的一邊是時尚的精品小店，另一邊則是老舊的中國餐館。這
　　　要怎麼形容？很衝突？

(Kari is pointing the restaurant Katz's Deli)

（凱莉指著一間叫做凱茲饗宴的餐廳。）

凱莉：一點也沒錯！這就是這一區美麗的地方，你有看過《當哈利遇見莎莉》這部電影
　　　嗎？他們有一場景是在這裡拍的。

單字說明　❶ 我們到了！　❷ 掃興的人　❸ 區域　❹ one... the other... 一個……另一個……（用於只描敘兩
　　　個事件時）　❺ 那叫什麼？要怎麼說？

艾凡：我聽說女神卡卡也是從這裡開始她的事業的。關於這個地方，我還有什麼應該要知道的嗎？

凱莉：我也是這麼聽說的！她以前在這裡的俱樂部表演。喜歡用便宜價錢買到好東西的買家會很享受在蘭花街商店購物的樂趣。

凱莉：除此之外，這區已經成為很多當代藝術藝廊的集散地。

凱莉：自從都市重建後，這區夜晚的治安已經改善很多，也變成了夜生活的好去處。

單字說明 ❶ 下東城（Lower East Side）的簡稱 ❷ 其它的／除此之外 ❸ 從前曾……（但現在不做了）❹ 喜歡想辦法以低價買得好商品的人 ❺ 除此之外（包括以上提到的，還有……）❻ 很多的 ❼ 當代的 ❽ 重建／改造 ❾ 目的地／去處

一定要知道的**單字**及**用語**！

跟著Kari和Ivan逛完下東城後，
別忘了繼續學習其它與本單元相關的道地美語常用單字及用語！

Halloween [ˌhælo`in]
萬聖節（俗稱的鬼節）

Kids play trick or treat on Halloween.
小朋友在萬聖節都會玩「不給糖就搗蛋」的遊戲。
（每年的萬聖節，下東城的鬼屋都會開放，讓民眾
進去體驗被驚嚇的樂趣。如果剛好在萬聖節前後拜
訪紐約，不妨去見識一下。）

numerous [`njumərəs] 很多的

He has numerous DVDs in his studio.
他的工作室裡有很多他收藏的DVD。

I am afraid (that)…
恐怕……

I am afraid (that) you have the
wrong number!
你恐怕打錯電話了！

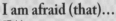

小補帖 **haunted** [`hɔntɪd] 鬧鬼的

People say that New Orleans is
the most haunted city in US.
有人說紐奧良是美國鬧鬼鬧最兇的城市。

excited about / over
對……感到很興奮、刺激

He is so excited about this trip.
他對這次的旅行感到很興奮。

Chapter **3**

點餐用餐、餐廳候位&問路的美式口語

taste [test] 嚐 / 嚐起來

Iced durians taste like ice cream.
冰過的榴槤吃起來像冰淇淋。

take place 發生 / 舉行

Joe's birthday party is taking place in his back yard.
喬的生日派對要在他的後院舉行。

area [ˋɛrɪə] 區域

This is a non-smoking area.
這裡是禁菸區。

perform [pɚˋfɔrm] 表演

Cindy is going to perform on TV next week.
辛蒂下禮拜要在電視上表演。

be in shape
維持好身材（或好狀態）

Jessie is in a great shape.
婕西把她的身材維持得很好。

chic [ˋʃik] 時髦的 / 時尚的

I saw Carrie the other day. She looked so chic!
我前天看到凱莉了，她看起來好時髦！

gentrified [ˈdʒɛntrɪfaɪd] 重建過的
They work very hard to have their hometown gentrified.
他們非常努力地重建家園。

☆
小補帖 **exactly** [ɪgˈzæktlɪ] 精確的 / 完全的
Do you know exactly where he is?
你知道他確切位置在哪嗎？

contemporary
[kənˈtɛmpəˌrɛrɪ] 當代的
Andy Warhol is a legendary contemporary artist.
安迪沃荷是一位傳奇的當代藝術家。

Andy Warhol

boutique [buˈtik] 高級精品店 / 女裝店
The dresses in boutique shop are a bit pricy.
在精品店裡的洋裝都有點貴。

I wish... 我希望……
小補帖 （加上過去式動詞時表示對不可能或與現實相反的希望）
I wish I could fly. 我希望我會飛。

點餐用餐、餐廳候位&問路的美式口語

Chapter **3**

來做練習吧！Let's practice

學習完本單元的單字及用語後，趕緊來做些練習，加深印象。

① Joe's birthday party is _____ _____ in his back yard.
喬的生日派對要在他的後院舉行。

② She _____ _____ perform at clubs here.
她以前在這裡的俱樂部表演。

③ The colors are so _____ !
用色好大膽！

④ People say that New Orleans is the most _____ city in US.
有人說紐奧良是美國鬧鬼鬧最兇的城市。

⑤ _____ _____ the passing trains on the next track make a lot of noise.
可惜經過隔壁鐵道的列車太吵了。

⑥ _____ _____ _____ (that) you have the wrong number!
你恐怕打錯電話了！

⑦ I see chic boutique shops on one side of the street and old Chinese restaurants on _____ _____ .
街道的一邊是時尚的精品小店，另一邊則是老舊的中國餐館。

⑧ Andy Warhol is a legendary _____ artist.
安迪沃荷是一位傳奇的當代藝術家。

⑨ Their pancakes _____ _____ No. 1 in New York!
他們的鬆餅被評為紐約第一！

⑩ Jessie _____ _____ a great _____ .
婕西把她的身材維持得很好。

解答
1. taking place 2. used to 3. bold 4. haunted
5. Too bad 6. I am afraid 7. the other 8. contemporary
9. are ranked 10. is in / shape

試穿、退換貨

Day 23 學習量：單字50個 / 會話用語40則

在金融區（Financial District）逛街，向專櫃人員詢問試穿及退換貨事宜

受朋友之託，艾凡來到位於金融區的二十一世紀百貨公司買過季的名牌商品！順便逛逛華爾街。

MP3 23

艾凡：我需要列一張表。我把每一樣物品都寫下來。首先，我要先幫自己找一件羽絨外套。

艾凡：這些對我來説都太大了。不好意思，請問這件有小一點的嗎？

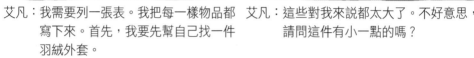

艾凡：請問試衣間在哪裡？我可以試穿這件襯衫嗎？

艾凡：請問這有別的顏色嗎？我在找比較正式，可以出席正式場合的衣服。

艾凡：請給我看最上排的那個紅色帽子。

單字說明　❶ 表 / 表單（亦可作動詞，為「列表」的意思）❷ write... down 把……寫下來
❸ big＜bigger＜biggest 大＜較大＜最大 / small＞smaller＞smallest 小＞較小＞最小 ❹ 試衣間
❺ try on 試穿 ❻ 需要 ❼ 場合 ❽ 排（top row 最上排 / front row 前排）

198

艾凡：這個手拿包的價錢真划算。包含稅金嗎？

艾凡：我在找皮夾克，你知道放在哪個走道嗎？

艾凡：這可以退貨嗎？可以幫我包裝成禮物嗎？

艾凡：喔，糟了！我沒有足夠現金，我可以用信用卡嗎？

艾凡：既然我都在這了，應該要去看一下華爾街的金牛。我也參觀了世貿中心的災變遺址。

Chapter 3
點餐用餐、餐廳候位&問路的美式口語

 單字說明　❶ 特價品 / 以便宜價錢買到的好商品　❷ 稅金　❸ 走道（seat by aisle 靠走道的位置）
❹ 可退貨的　❺ 禮物　❻ 包裝　❼ 信用卡　❽ check out 看看究竟 / 檢查　❾ 華爾街金牛
❿ 世貿中心災變遺址

I saw the famous ❶ Trinity Church on my left hand side. I took many photos of it.

艾凡：我看到鼎鼎有名的三一教堂在我左手邊。我照了很多它的照片。

I was ❷ headed toward South Street Sea Port, a popular spot to see Brooklyn Bridge from a different angle.❸

艾凡：我往南街碼頭走去，這是從另一個角度看布魯克林橋的熱門景點。

Walking ❹ with my hands full makes me exhausted. On top of that, ❺ I got lost on my way back.❻

艾凡：雙手拿滿東西行走搞得我快累死了。更慘的是，我還在回來的路上迷路了。

I decide to take a taxi home. I hail a taxi.❼

艾凡：我決定搭計程車回家。我攔住了一台計程車。

I feel ❽ upset because the taxi driver made a ❾ detour. It's been a long day!

艾凡：我心情很差，因為計程車司機繞路了。這真是漫長累人的一天。

 ❶ 三一教堂（紐約華爾街上很有名的天主教堂） ❷ head to / toward 往……方向去 ❸ 角度 ❹ 表示……狀態 ❺ get / be lost 迷路 ❻ on the way back 回程路上 ❼ 攔計程車 ❽ 沮喪 / 不開心 ❾ 繞路

一定要知道的**單字及用語**！

跟著Kari和Ivan逛完金融區後，
別忘了繼續學習其它與本單元相關的道地美語常用單字及用語！

on my way back 在我回程的路上
I grabbed a cup of coffee on my way back.
我在回程的路上順便買了一杯咖啡。

shoot [ʃut] 糟了！（shit的委婉用詞）
Shoot! I left my cell phone at the café.
糟糕！我把手機忘在咖啡店了！
🔁 darn（damn的委婉用詞）
heck（hell的委婉用詞）

banquet [ˋbæŋkwɪt]
宴會／盛宴
We are having a banquet for grandma's birthday.
我們將為外婆舉辦一個生日宴會。

get lost 迷路
I got lost when I visited Mr. Smith.
我拜訪史密斯先生的時候迷路了。

take a photo of...
照⋯⋯的照片

I took many photos of their baby.
我幫他們的寶寶照了很多照片。
take photos for... 為⋯⋯拍照

exhausted [ɪgˋzɔstɪd]
累到快要虛脫的狀態
After a 12-hour flight, I am exhausted.
經過十二小時的飛行，我已經快累死了。

小補帖 **on top of that** 更糟的是／更棒的是
（表示比前一情況更嚴重的連接詞，好或壞的情況皆可用）
He is not friendly at all; on top of that, he hates me.
他已經不是很友善了，更慘的是，他還討厭我。

receipt [rɪ`sit] 收據 / 發票

You can get a full refund in 30 days with your receipt.
持收據三十天內可全額退款。

invoice [`ɪnvɔɪs]
明細 / 發票

Please check the quantity on the latest invoice.
請檢查最新一張明細表的數量。

return policy 退換貨規則

return [rɪ`tɜn] 退（貨）

I'd like to return this pair of jeans.
我想要退這條牛仔褲。

blouse [blaʊz] 女用襯衫

tank-top [`tæŋktɑp]
坦克背心

sweater [`swɛtɚ] 毛衣

vest [vɛst] 背心

shorts [ʃɔrts] 短褲

down jacket
羽絨外套（down 羽絨）

item [ˈaɪtəm] 物品 / 物件
We have a 6-item limit for fitting room.
我們更衣室規定最多只能帶六件物品。

find [faɪnd] 找 / 找尋
I can't find my sweater.
我找不到我的毛衣。

formal [ˈfɔrml̩] 正式的
Jack is dressed formally for the wedding.
傑克穿得很正式參加婚禮。

Chapter **3** 點餐用餐、餐廳候位&問路的美式口語

Hoodie [ˈhʊdɪ] 帽T

blazer [ˈblezɚ] 西裝外套

cardigan [ˈkɑrdɪgən] 針織衫

小補帖 **casual** [ˈkæʒuəl] 休閒的 / 不拘禮節的

來做練習吧！Let's practice

學習完本單元的單字及用語後，趕緊來做些練習，加深印象。

❶ You can get a full refund in 30 days with your ＿＿＿＿＿＿ .

持收據三十天內可全額退款。

❷ I'd like to ＿＿＿＿＿＿ this pair of jeans.

我想要退這條牛仔褲。

❸ Can I use my ＿＿＿＿＿＿ ＿＿＿＿＿＿ ?

我可以用信用卡嗎？

❹ I decide to take a taxi home. I ＿＿＿＿＿＿ a taxi.

我決定搭計程車回家。我攔住了一台計程車。

❺ Can I ＿＿＿＿＿＿ this shirt ＿＿＿＿＿＿ ?

我可以試穿這件襯衫嗎？

❻ Where is the ＿＿＿＿＿＿ ＿＿＿＿＿＿ ?

請問試衣間在哪裡？

❼ I grab a cup of coffee ＿＿＿＿＿＿ ＿＿＿＿＿＿ ＿＿＿＿＿＿ ＿＿＿＿＿＿ .

我在回程的路上順便買了一杯咖啡。

❽ He is not friendly at all; ＿＿＿＿＿＿ ＿＿＿＿＿＿ ＿＿＿＿＿＿ ＿＿＿＿＿＿ , he hates me.

他已經不是很友善了，更慘的是，他還討厭我。

❾ Is this ＿＿＿＿＿＿ ?

這可以退貨嗎？

❿ This clutch is a real ＿＿＿＿＿＿ .

這個手拿包的價錢真划算。

解答

1.receipt 2. return 3. credit card 4. hail 5. try / on
6. fitting room 7. on my way back 8. on top of that
9. returnable 10. bargain

Chapter 4

其它日常生活中
會用到的美式口語

在布魯克林區（Brooklyn）學習其它與日常生活相
關的用語

參加派對注意事項

準備到威廉斯堡（Williamsburg）參加朋友的派對

美食、音樂、創意，威廉斯堡一樣不缺！享受Juliette和Egg的戶外早午餐，SEA的泰式風味，Fornino無人可比的披薩藝術和藏在巷弄間的創意市集！或到布魯克林保齡球場來一場保齡球大戰，來到威廉斯堡，「無聊」是一項不可思議的奢侈。

MP3 24

凱莉：你記得我朋友朱利安嗎？

艾凡：記得啊！上禮拜在曼哈頓橋下通行區巧遇的那一位。

凱莉：對啊！他要回歐洲去了，辦了一個歡送派對！你可以陪我去嗎？

艾凡：好啊！那我要帶些什麼嗎？

凱莉：他的邀請函寫「酒類自備」，而且你必須要戴上帽子！那是派對的衣著限制。

艾凡：哈哈，真有趣！真有他的風格！

 ❶ bump into someone 巧遇某人 ❷ 歡送派對（farewell 告別） ❸ 在這指參加派對的伴

❹ 邀請函 ❺ 酒類、酒精類飲料（口語講法）

His ❶loft is located in Williamsburg. I am thinking about going to Fornino ❷on the way.

The pizzeria you've been talking about? I've been wanting to go!

FORNINO

凱莉：他的公寓在威廉斯堡那一帶。我想順便去吃附近的Fornino披薩。

艾凡：你一直提到的那家嗎？我一直好想去！

Go downstairs and hail a ❸cab. We are already late!

Try not to ❹linger! I don't wanna miss the pizza.

凱莉：你先到樓下去招計程車吧！我們已經來不及了！

艾凡：不要搞太久喔，我不想錯過那披薩！

I forgot to tell you, there is a famous second-hand shop called Beacon's Closet.

becon's closet
buy . sell .trade .clothe

The people here all look very trendy.❺

凱莉：我忘了告訴你，這裡有一間非常有名的二手衣店，叫做「畢肯的衣櫥」。

艾凡：這一區的人看起來都好有型。

 單字說明　❶ 由倉庫或工廠改建而成的公寓　❷ 順道　❸ 攔計程車　❹ 拖拖拉拉　❺ 很時髦的

Yeah, this neighborhood has been rated the youngest and most creative area. Many artists ①choose to live here.

We ②should have come here earlier. I wish we had enough time to walk around.

Maybe next time! Julian would be ③upset if we stood him up④

True! I don't want to piss him off.

凱莉：對啊！這裡被評為最年輕最有創意一區！很多藝術家都住在這。

艾凡：天吶！我們應該早點來的！我真希望有時間可以好好逛一逛。

凱莉：下次吧！如果我們放朱利安鴿子，他會很生氣的。

艾凡：這倒是！我可不想惹惱他！

⑤Vendors will be full of this street on weekends.

Unlike Manhattan, this area has this old New York style.

凱莉：到了週末，這裡排滿整條街的小攤販。

艾凡：和曼哈頓不同的是，這裡更多了一種舊紐約的感覺。

This place may look ⑥ghetto at the first ⑦glance, but once you dig in, it actually has a modern inside.

I already fell in love with it here.

凱莉：是啊！這個第一眼看起來很像貧民區的地方，其實藏了很多時髦的東西呢！

艾凡：我想我已經愛上這裡了。

單字說明 ❶ 選擇 ❷ 早該……（指過去的事）❸ 不開心／心煩意亂 ❹ 放……鴿子 ❺ 小攤販
❻ 猶太人區／貧民區／老舊的地方 ❼ 一瞥

一定要知道的**單字及用語**！

跟著Kari和Ivan逛完威廉斯堡後，
別忘了繼續學習其它與本單元相關的道地美語常用單字及用語！

INFORMATION

safe flight
當朋友需要搭機遠行時，用來祝福對方
一切順利

You have a safe flight, honey! Give me a call
when you arrive in HK.
一路順風，親愛的！到了香港給我個電話。

… from now ……以後

I am going to LA 7 days from now.
我七天之後要去洛杉磯。

… later ……以後（只能用在過去式）

I went to Chicago 3 months later and then came here.
三個月之後，我去了芝加哥然後再來這裡。

run into 撞見／撞到

I ran into Marian yesterday. She looked great.
我昨天碰到瑪麗安，她看起來很好。

 the other day 前幾天

小補帖

Sam came by the other day and left us some
home-made cookies.
山姆前幾天來，而且還留了自己做的餅乾給我們。

sure thing 當然啊！（通常用於回答）

A: Can you give me a copy of this information?
B: Sure thing.
A：這些資訊你可以影印一份給我嗎？
B：當然。

小補帖 **keep one's promise** 遵守諾言

You don't have to worry. She always keeps her promise.
不用擔心啦，她一向很遵守諾言。

小補帖 **cancel on someone** 取消跟某人的約會

She will be angry if I cancel on her.
如果我取消了跟她的約會，她一定會生我的氣。

a whole pizza pie
一整個不切的披薩

I would like a whole pizza pie to go, plain!
我要外帶一整個披薩，原味的！

slice [slaɪs] 一片

I had a slice of pepperoni pizza for lunch.
我今天吃了一片臘腸披薩當午餐。

booth [buθ]（售票）亭 / 攤

Ian is at the ticket booth buying tickets.
伊恩正在售票亭買票。

invite [ɪn`vaɪt] 邀請

I hope you don't mind that I invited Kim
to my birthday party.
希望你不要介意我邀請了金來參加我的生日派對。

junk shop 二手雜貨店（非慈善目的）

Sometimes, he finds really good stuff at junk shops.
有時候他在二手商店也能找到好東西。

brewery [ˋbruərɪ] 釀啤酒廠

You'll see many small breweries in Williamsburg.
在威廉斯堡，可以看到很多小的釀啤酒廠。

thrift shop 二手商店（慈善目的）

That thrift shop at the corner donates their income to help children in need.
轉角那間二手慈善商店把營收捐給需要的小孩。

liquor store 酒類專賣店

I got you a bottle of wine from the liquor store downstairs.
我從樓下的酒類專賣店買了一瓶酒給你。

ice cream truck 冰淇淋車

🈺 紐約和很多其它城市在夏天時，路上到處可見冰淇淋車，有霜淇淋和雪糕類，口味很多！最近也有很多標榜高品質和天然材料的冰淇淋加入戰局，有機會的話不妨嚐一嚐。

scoop [skup] 一球（冰淇淋）

The boy has two scoops of ice cream on his little hand.
那個小男孩的小手裡握了兩球冰淇淋。

cone [kon] 冰淇淋筒／圓錐狀的物品

Would you like your ice cream on cone or cup?
你冰淇淋要裝甜筒還是杯子？

其它日常生活中會用到的美式口語　Chapter 4

來做練習吧！Let's practice

學習完本單元的單字及用語後，趕緊來做些練習，加深印象。

❶ Yes, I do! We _____ _____ him in Dumbo last week.
記得啊！上禮拜在曼哈頓橋下通行區巧遇的那一位。

❷ Maybe next time! Julian would be upset if we _____ _____ _____ .

下次吧！如果我們放朱利安鴿子，他會很生氣的。

❸ Go downstairs and _____ _____ _____ . We are already late!
你先到樓下去招計程車吧！我們已經來不及了！

❹ The boy has two _____ of ice cream on his little hand.
那個小男孩的小手裡握了兩球冰淇淋。

❺ Sam came by _____ _____ _____ and left us some home-made cookies.
山姆前幾天有來，而且還留了自己做的餅乾給我們。

❻ I had a _____ of pepperoni pizza for lunch.
我今天吃了一片臘腸披薩當午餐。

❼ He is going back to Europe and is gonna throw a _____ _____ !
他要回歐洲去了，辦了一個歡送派對！

❽ You don't have to worry. She always _____ _____ _____ .
不用擔心啦，她一向很遵守諾言。

❾ Would you like your ice cream on _____ or cup?
你冰淇淋要裝甜筒還是杯子？

❿ This place may look ghetto at the first _____ , but once you dig in, it actually has a modern inside.
是啊！這個第一眼看起來很像貧民區的地方，其實藏了很多時髦的東西呢！

解答

1. bumped into 2. stood him up 3. hail a cab 4. scoops
5. the other day 6. slice 7. farewell party
8. keeps her promise 9. cone 10. glance

安慰失意的朋友

用布魯克林高地步行區（Brooklyn Height Promenade）的風景撫慰受傷的心靈

不管多繁忙的城市，都會有一個安靜的角落，讓你靜靜地以旁觀者的角度看著城市裡的繁忙！跟著凱莉和艾凡一起到布魯克林高地步行區把壞心情丟掉吧！

MP3 25

I must have **gotten** up on the wrong side of the bed!❶

What's up? You sound **depressed**.❷

凱莉：今天不知道倒了什麼霉！
艾凡：怎麼了？你聽起來很沮喪。

❸I don't **wanna** talk about that!

Come on! I'll show you something! Something beautiful and free!

凱莉：唉！別說了！
艾凡：走！我帶你去看個東西！很漂亮而且不用花錢！

Uh...sorry, but I kind of❹ **prefer** just stay at home and **kick back**!❺

Just this once, trust me, okay?

凱莉：嗯⋯⋯可是我其實比較想待在家放鬆就好！
艾凡：就這麼一次，相信我！好嗎？

Haha! I am ❻**all yours**, sir!

Get dressed. Departing time at 3:00 **sharp**!❼

凱莉：哈哈，一切都聽你的！長官。
艾凡：準備著裝，出發時間訂為三點整，準時！

單字說明　❶（俚語）今天真倒楣 / 諸事不順　❷ 沮喪 / 情緒低落　❸ 我現在不想談 / 我不想說　❹ 寧願　❺ 放鬆 / 平靜下來　❻ 悉聽尊便 / 都聽你的　❼ 加在時間後，表示「強調要準時、分秒不差」

(on the train)

Do you wanna talk about it now? Or should I keep my mouth shut?❶❷

Well... I flunked my art history!

（在地鐵上）
艾凡：你現在想談一談了嗎？還是我應該閉嘴？
凱莉：嗯……其實是我的美術史被當掉了！

❸How come? You bust your butt❹ day in and day out.

I did, didn't I? But I am so darn stupid to forget today my final report is due. So...

艾凡：怎麼會？我看你唸得很認真啊。
凱莉：就是説啊！但我竟然忘記今天就是我期末報告的截止日！所以……

❺Sorry for the pause! But I don't know what to say!

I know! I have only myself to blame!

艾凡：我知道我應該安慰你，但我真的不知道該説什麼。
凱莉：我懂！我只能怪自己。

其它日常生活中會用到的美式口語

Chapter 4

Get yourself ❶off the hook! It is not the end of the world. Leave your sadness on Manhattan Island! We are now all the way in Brooklyn.

艾凡：看開點！這又不是世界末日。把你的不開心留在曼哈頓島上吧！我們現在遠在布魯克林呢！

You are right! The ❷skyline is spectacular!❸ It looks like another world from here.

Here! I grabbed your favorite chocolate bar on the way out!

凱莉：沒錯！這天際線真的好美！從這裡看起來好像是另一個世界。
艾凡：這給你，我出來的時後順手拿了你最喜歡的巧克力棒。

Oh! That's so very ❹sweet of you! I feel so much better now.

Don't forget to talk to your teacher tomorrow! I'll keep my fingers crossed for you!

凱莉：你真好！我現在感覺好多了！
艾凡：別忘了明天找老師談一談！我會幫你祈禱的！

單字說明 ❶ 放過、擺脫困境 ❷ 天際線／由岸邊建築物所構成的連線 ❸ 壯麗的／驚人美麗的 ❹ 你非常貼心（等於very nice of you）

一定要知道的**單字及用語**！

跟著Kari和Ivan逛完布魯克林高地步行區後，
別忘了繼續學習其它與本單元相關的道地美語常用單字及用語！

 neon light 霓虹燈

Do you see the neon light on top of that building?
你有看到那棟大樓頂端的霓虹燈嗎？

depart [dɪ`part] 出發 / 離開

The flight to Taipei has departed.
往台北的班機已經飛走囉。

night view 夜景

The beautiful night view comforts me.
這美麗的夜景安撫了我。

report [rɪ`port] 報告

The weather report says tomorrow will be a sunny day.
氣象報告說，明天是大晴天。

take off 起飛 / 離開

Hey! I am taking off. See you at school.
我要先走囉，學校見。

Please fasten your seat belts. We are about to take off.
請繫緊安全帶，我們即將起飛。

forget to V 忘了去做……
forget V-ing 忘了做過……

I forget to buy the tickets!
我忘記買票了！

I forget buying the tickets.
我忘了我已經買好票了。

219

I have only myself to blame!
我只能怪自己 / 自作自受

I should have studied harder.
I have only myself to blame!
我當時應該用功點，現在只能怪自己了！

upset [ʌpˋsɛt] 鬱悶的 / 不開心的

Why are you upset? You made your own bed.
你幹嘛不高興？這是你自找的。

feel blue 覺得憂鬱

sad [sæd] 傷心 / 悲傷

down [daʊn] 鬱悶 / 提不起勁

flunk [flʌŋk] 不及格 / 被當掉

Jim flunked his math this semester
and he regretted.
吉姆這學期的數學被當掉了，他很後悔。

thrilled [θrɪld] 狂喜的
excited [ɪkˋsaɪtɪd] 興奮的

anxious [ˋæŋkʃəs] 因緊張或期待而焦慮的
nervous [ˋnɝvəs] 緊張的

presentation [͵prizɛnˋteʃən]
口頭報告／展示

Everyone is going to do a presentation when this course is finished.
這課程結束後，大家都要上台做口頭報告。

deadline [ˋdɛd͵laɪn] 截止日／最後期限

The deadline of application is on 3/23.
三月二十三日是申請的截止日。

assignment [əˋsaɪnmənt]
指派的工作／作業

homework [ˋhom͵wɜk] 回家作業

for (this) once 就（這麼）一次

For once, she is making her point.
就這麼一次，她總算講到重點了。

stay up 熬夜

I stayed up all night for this exam.
為了這次考試我一整晚沒睡。

keep the fingers crossed 祈禱

Hope it will be sunny day on my wedding day!
I'll keep my fingers crossed.
希望我婚禮當天是個大晴天！我衷心祈禱。

其它日常生活中會用到的美式口語 Chapter 4

來做練習吧！Let's practice

學習完本單元的單字及用語後，趕緊來做些練習，加深印象。

① Jim _____ his math this semester and he regretted.

吉姆這學期的數學被當掉了，他很後悔。

② I _____ _____ all night for this exam.

為了這次考試我一整晚沒睡。

③ You sound _____ .

你聽起來很沮喪。

④ The skyline is _____ ! It looks like another world from here.

這天際線真的好美！從這裡看起來好像是另一個世界。

⑤ You _____ _____ _____ day in and day out.

我看你唸得很認真啊。

⑥ I _____ _____ _____ the tickets!

我忘記買票了！

⑦ I _____ _____ the tickets.

我忘了我已經買好票了。

⑧ I must have gotten up on the _____ _____ of the bed!

今天不知道倒了什麼霉！

⑨ That's so _____ _____ _____ you!

你真好！

⑩ Hope it will be sunny day on my wedding day! I'll _____ _____

_____ _____ .

希望我婚禮當天是個大晴天！我衷心祈禱。

解答

1. flunked 2. stayed up 3. depressed 4. spectacular
5. bust your butt 6. forget to buy 7. forget buying
8. wrong side 9. very sweet of
10. keep my fingers crossed

野餐去！

Day 26 學習量：單字70個 / 會話用語35則

到布魯克林植物園（Brooklyn Botanic Garden）賞櫻、野餐

每年的三四月份櫻花盛開，但可別以為只有在東京才有賞花季！今天凱莉和艾凡就準備到布魯克林植物園好好享受美麗的櫻花和美味的野餐。

MP3 26

Wake up! We have a lunch box to prepare.

凱莉：趕快起床，我們得準備午餐的餐盒呢。

Okay, I'll get some cheese and ham.

艾凡：好！我先去買些起司和火腿。

Could you get me some heavy cream and peanut butter? And fruit too! Thanks!

Call me if you need anything else!

凱莉：可以幫我買一些鮮奶油和花生醬嗎？還有水果！謝囉！
艾凡：沒問題！如果有需要其他的，你再打給我！

You gotta have it done in half an hour! We should be taking off at 10.

No worries, you will be ❶ dazed by my ❷ punctuality.

凱莉：你半小時內要買完喔！我們十點要出發。
艾凡：別擔心！我會準時到讓你驚訝！

單字說明 ❶ 昏眩 ❷ 準時

凱莉：好了，我們都準備好了！走吧！
艾凡：啊！等我一下！我的地鐵票卡到期了。

（到了植物園裡）
凱莉：人好多喔！你有國際學生證嗎？可以打折。

艾凡：有啊！你在這裡等我！我去買票就
　　　好了。

凱莉：你看！這邊有地圖！我們要去那裡。

單字說明　❶ 塞爆的／擁擠的

225

凱莉：等等！這個牛奶好像壞掉了。
艾凡：嗯！聞起來怪怪的！丟掉好了。

凱莉：這是我到上城買的鮭魚沙拉，它超好吃！
艾凡：不要跟我說這是從Barney Greengrass買的！可以給我吃一口嗎？

凱莉：不知道為什麼我還是餓耶！等等到卜派吃頓大餐吧。
艾凡：好啊！他們的炸雞和比斯吉真是超級好吃。

單字說明 ❶ 牛奶酸敗

一定要知道的**單字及用語**！

跟著Kari和Ivan逛完布魯克林植物園後，
別忘了繼續學習其它與本單元相關的道地美語常用單字及用語！

have... done 把……完成
I will have the translation done by Wednesday.
我星期三之前會把這些翻譯都完成。

小補帖 **in time** 及時

be all set
準備好了 / 辦好了
We are all set, Sir!
先生，所有程序都辦好了！

on time 準時
He always come to
work on time.
他總是準時上班。

小補帖 **else** [ɛls] 其他的
I don't know him,
but I know everyone else.
我不認識他，但其他人我都認識。

metro card 地鐵票

single ride 單程票

refill [ri`fɪl] 儲值

小補帖 **token** [`tokən] 代幣　　小補帖 **unlimited** [ʌn`lɪmɪtɪd] 月票（三十天內不限次數）

valid [ˋvælɪd] 有效的

This is a valid coupon.
You can use it to get a free combo.
這張折價券仍可使用，
你可以用來換一份免費的套餐。

offer [ˋɔfɚ] 提供

This diner offers 24-hr free coffee.
這間小餐館提供二十四小時免費咖啡。

小補帖 **ripe** [raɪp]（水果、作物）成熟了

（反義字：unripe）

The bananas are already ripe.
這些香蕉都熟了。

expired [ɪkˋspaɪrd] 過期了 / 失效了

The expired date of my credit card
is May 5th, 2012.
我的信用卡到期日為二○一二年五月五日。

rotten [ˋratṇ] 食物腐壞

The fish is rotten.
這魚已經餿掉了。

yum [jʌm]
好吃！

picnic [ˋpɪknɪk] 野餐
We had a picnic in Central Park yesterday.
我們昨天去中央公園野餐。

lunch box 午餐飯盒 / 便當
I have a tuna sandwich in my lunch box.
我的便當裡有一個鮪魚三明治。

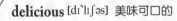

delicious [dɪˋlɪʃəs] 美味可口的
Sue makes delicious meals. I enjoy being her guest.
蘇做得一手好菜，我很享受到她家作客。

Can I have a bite? 我可以吃一口嗎？
Can I have a sip? 我可以喝一口嗎？

小補帖 **heavy cream**
重奶油（通常為做料理用的奶油）

小補帖 **whipped cream**
鮮奶油（打發起泡的奶油）

小補帖 **butter** [ˋbʌtɚ] 牛油

其它日常生活中會用到的美式口語

Chapter 4

來做練習吧！ Let's practice

學習完本單元的單字及用語後，趕緊來做些練習，加深印象。

❶ This place is _____ !

人好多喔！

❷ _____ _____ , you will be dazed by my punctuality.

別擔心！我會準時到讓你驚訝！

❸ I have a tuna sandwich in my _____ _____ .

我的便當裡有一個鮪魚三明治。

❹ The bananas are already _____ .

這些香蕉都熟了。

❺ The fish is _____ .

這魚已經餿掉了。

❻ Wait! I think the milk is _____ .

等等！這個牛奶好像壞掉了。

❼ Okay, we _____ _____ _____ !

好了，我們都準備好了！

❽ This is a _____ coupon. You can use it to get a free combo.

這張折價券仍可使用，你可以用來換一份免費的套餐。

❾ The _____ date of my credit card is May 5th, 2012.

我的信用卡到期日為二〇一二年五月五日。

❿ He always come to work _____ _____ .

他總是準時上班。

解答

1. jammed 2. No worries 3. lunch box 4. ripe 5. rotten
6. spoiled 7. are all set 8. valid 9. expired
10. on time

我喉嚨痛，還流鼻水

出發前往曼哈頓橋下通行區（Dumbo）前發現身體不舒服…

週末早上，艾凡看著電影《紐約我愛你》，突然發現了一個他前所未見的場景，一問之下，原來在藝術氣息濃厚的曼哈頓橋下。艾凡正想邀凱莉一起去時，卻發現凱莉臉色蒼白……

MP3 27

艾凡：凱莉，你有看過《紐約我愛你》這部電影嗎？
凱莉：有啊！怎麼了？

艾凡：那你記不記得娜塔莉波曼和她老公碰面的那個場景？
凱莉：喔！那在Dumbo區的公園。

艾凡：Dumbo？我不知道這個地方！
凱莉：Dumbo是「曼哈頓橋下通行區」的
　　　縮寫！在布魯克林。

艾凡：那個地方怎麼樣啊？是很多黑人的
　　　地方嗎？
凱莉：人家說那是第二個威廉斯堡，年輕
　　　藝術家的另一個天堂。

單字說明 ❶ 指黑人很多的地方，有時也指治安很差的區域 ❷ 天堂

艾凡：我想那應該值得我跑一趟親自去看看，你要一起去嗎？
凱莉：謝謝你邀請我，但是我今天不太舒服。

艾凡：你還好吧？你臉色看起來很蒼白。

凱莉：我還好，只是我想我今天應該會在家
待著然後好好休息。

艾凡：如果你需要什麼幫忙，再告訴我！
凱莉：別讓我耽誤你了！曼哈頓橋下是個很藝術的區域，你會喜歡那裡的。

單字說明 ❶ 親自 / 親眼 ❷ 通常用在謝謝對方詢問，尤其是問候身體狀況，家庭狀況或者是提出邀請時
❸ 臉色蒼白的 ❹ 悠閒地度過時間 ❺ 有藝術氣息的

Wait! Jacques Torres Chocolate is a must!❶ Don't forget to give yourself a treat❷.

凱莉：等等！Jacques Torres巧克力店是一個你非去不可的點，別忘了給你自己一點甜頭！

This area sure looks like Williamsburg, very slow yet energetic.

艾凡：這裡看起來還真像威廉斯堡，步調雖然緩慢卻很有活力。

Sir, this is a ❸forbidden area! You are not allowed to go through.❹

I am sorry! I didn't see the post.

DO NOT ENTER

警察：先生，這裡是禁區喔！你不能從這邊通過。
艾凡：不好意思，我剛剛沒有看到那張告示。

(murmuring) A movie will be shooting in an hour; maybe I'll see some movie stars over here. This is the first time for me to see a ❺professional movie shoot❻. New York is a city full of surprises.

艾凡：（喃喃自語地説）一個小時後有電影要在這邊拍攝，我搞不好可以看到一些電影明星耶！這是我第一次看到專業的電影拍攝，紐約真是一個充滿驚喜的城市！

  ❶ 非去不可的地方／非做不可的事 ❷ 甜點 ❸ 禁止的／管制的 ❹ 通過 ❺ 專業的 ❻ 拍攝

一定要知道的**單字及用語**！

跟著Kari和Ivan逛完Dumbo後，
別忘了繼續學習其它與本單元相關的道地美語常用單字及用語！

dangerous [ˈdendʒərəs] 危險的

Harlem is a rather dangerous area.
Don't go there alone at late night.
哈林區是比較危險的區域，
晚上不要一個人去那裡。

sign [saɪn] 標示

Turn left at the first traffic sign and
then you will see a 7-eleven.
第一個紅綠燈左轉，你就會看到一間7-eleven超商。

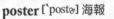

permission [pəˈmɪʃən] 允許 / 通行證

You are not allowed to get in without
the owner's permission.
沒有持有者的允許，你是不可以進去的。

poster [ˈpostə] 海報

I bought a Titanic movie poster when
I was in middle school.
我國中的時候買了一張鐵達尼號的電影海報。

join [dʒɔɪn] 參加 / 加入

We are going to visit Mr. Wang.
Do you want to join us?
我們要去拜訪王先生，你要不要加入我們？

postcard [ˈpostˌkɑrd] 明信片

I send a postcard to myself once I arrive a new place.
只要到新的地方，我都會寄一張明信片給自己。

 in + 時間 在……時間內

Simon is leaving for Europe in 2 weeks.
賽門兩個禮拜後要去歐洲。

Chapter **4**
其它日常生活中會用到的美式口語

medication [ˌmɛdɪˋkeʃən] 藥方 / 藥

Have you taken your medication today?
你今天吃藥了嗎？

sore throat
喉嚨痛

migraine
[ˋmaɪgren]
偏頭痛

小補帖 **ill** [ɪl] 生病 / 不舒服

pill [pɪl] 藥丸（單用時常指避孕藥）

The yellow pills are very useful
for heartburn.
這些黃色的小藥丸對於胃灼熱很有效。

food poisoning
食物中毒

diarrhea
[ˌdaɪəˋriə]
腹瀉

runny nose
流鼻水

allergy
[ˋælədʒɪ]
過敏

pale [pel] 臉色蒼白

She looked pale when she got off the train.
她從火車上下來的時候臉色很蒼白。

stomachache
[ˋstʌmək͵ek] 胃痛

under the weather 身體不舒服

I felt under the weather in the morning, so I didn't go into work.
我早上不太舒服，所以就沒去上班了！

 kick back 放鬆

I am going to just stay home and kick back this weekend.
我這個週末只想要待在家好好放鬆。

scene [sin] 場景

I've seen this scene for many times in movies.
我在電影裡常常看到這個場景。

小補帖 **downtown** [ˌdaunˋtaun] 市區

（downtown這個字本指市區，但因為紐約市的分區較特殊，故在紐約稱為下城區。）

We went downtown to see a movie last weekend.
我們上週末去市區看電影。

showroom [ˋʃoˌrum] 展示間 / 展示區

I picked up some dresses from their showroom.
我從他們的展示間挑了幾件洋裝。

bit [bɪt] 一點點 / 一些

The sauce is a little bit too spicy for me.
那個醬汁對我來說有點太辣了。

其它日常生活中會用到的美式口語

Chapter **4**

studio [ˋstjudɪo]
個人工作室（或指無隔間的單房公寓套房）

I am looking for a one-bedroom, not a studio.
我要找的是一房一廳的，不是套房。

小補帖 **Don't let me stop you.**
別因為我而不去（做）
別為我放棄大好機會

Don't let me stop you. I'll catch you up later.
別因為我停下來，我等等會追上你！

Don't let me stop you. New York is where you've always wanted to go.
別為我放棄這個機會，你一直很想去紐約的。

來做練習吧！Let's practice

學習完本單元的單字及用語後，趕緊來做些練習，加深印象。

1 I felt _____ _____ _____ in the morning, so I didn't go into work.

我早上不太舒服，所以就沒去上班了！

2 I picked up some dresses from their _____ .

我從他們的展示間挑了幾件洋裝。

3 I think it's worth a trip to see this place _____ _____ .

我想那應該值得我跑一趟親自去看看。

4 Sir, this is a _____ area!

先生，這裡是禁區喔！

5 I am fine! I think I am just gonna _____ _____ here and take a rest.

我還好，只是我想我今天應該會在家待著然後好好休息。

6 She looked _____ when she got off the train.

她從火車上下來的時候臉色很蒼白。

7 I am looking for a one-bedroom, not a _____ .

我要找的是一房一廳的，不是套房。

8 Would you like to _____ me?

你要一起去嗎？

9 People say it is the next Williamsburg, another _____ for young artists.

人家說那是第二個威廉斯堡，年輕藝術家的另一個天堂。

10 I send a _____ to myself once I arrive a new place.

只要到新的地方，我都會寄一張明信片給自己。

解答

1. under the weather 2. showroom 3. in person
4. forbidden 5. hang out 6. pale 7. studio 8. join
9. paradise 10. postcard

量販店、藥妝店、零售雜貨店的差別

Day 28 學習量：單字60個 / 會話用語40則

參加布魯克林博物館（Brooklyn Museum）的派對，順道
逛逛大西洋大道（Atlantic Avenue）上的零售雜貨店

試過在博物館裡狂歡嗎？來布魯克林博物館隨著現場表演的DJ一起跳舞吧！順
便還可以和凱莉一起去逛逛大西洋大道上的個性小店，這裡可是有時尚大師的
祕密基地喔！

MP3 28

艾凡：哇！你看起來超正，你要出去嗎？
凱莉：對啊，我要去布魯克林博物館。

艾凡：博物館？你看起來比較像要去參加
　　　派對吧！
凱莉：其實是啊！

艾凡：辦在博物館的派對？你認真的嗎？
凱莉：每個月的第一個禮拜六都有辦派對！
　　　免費入場！

凱莉：你乾脆和我一起去吧！
艾凡：這個派對難道不是只有被邀請的人才能進去嗎？

單字說明　❶ 美到翻天的　❷ yes的可愛講法　❸ 你何不跟我一起去呢？（雖是問句形式，更像是邀請）
❹ 有受邀才能進入

凱莉：不需要邀請函啊！你趕快去打扮一下，我們還可以去大西洋大道買點東西。
艾凡：好耶，布魯克林一夜遊！我要去！

凱莉：時間還早，我們在這裡下車去Target逛逛吧！
艾凡：Target？你確定要在去派對之前買日用品？

凱莉：哈哈！Target可不只賣雜貨喔，他們很努力地創造出自己的特色。
艾凡：他們怎麼做到的？

單字說明　❶ 盛裝打扮　❷ 我很有興趣　❸ 美國第五大零售商，販賣的物品繁多，舉凡日用品、傢俱、服飾、零食……等　❹ 賣各種雜貨的商場　❺ 特色／特徵　❻ 他們怎麼辦到的？（口語用法）

Have you heard of Zac Posen, Anna Sui, Marc Jacobs? They are all high-end fashion designers. Target has ❶cooperated with them to ❷launch a series called "XXX for Target."

MARC JACOBS

ZAC POSEN

ANNA SUI

Which means you can have the high-end ❸design with affordable prices?

凱莉：你有聽過查克波森、安娜蘇、馬克賈伯嗎？這些都是設計高級服飾的時裝設計師。Target 找這些設計師合作，推出了一個叫做「XXX for Target」的聯名系列。

艾凡：意思就是，你可以用負擔得起的價格買到高級設計師的設計？

Exactly! Shall we ❹dig in now?

Of course! I also ❺noticed there are so many ❻attractive boutique shops around.

凱莉：一點也沒錯！那我們現在可以進去一探究竟了嗎？

艾凡：當然囉！我剛剛一路上也看到了很多很吸引我的精品小店。

We'd better hurry then!

TARGET
CHUCKE CHEESE'S
OAFFY'S
ATLANTIC TERMINAL
TARGET

凱莉：那我們最好動作快點！

242　單字說明　❶ 合作　❷ 推出 / 發行　❸ 負擔得起的　❹ 深入了解　❺ 注意到　❻ 有吸引力的 / 吸引人的

一定要知道的**單字及用語**！

跟著Kari和Ivan逛完布魯克林博物館後，
別忘了繼續學習其它與本單元相關的道地美語常用單字及用語！

new arrivals 新品上架

We have new arrivals on the front rack.
我們的新產品都在前面的架上。

high-end [haɪˋɛnd] 高價的 / 高級的

Our company is going to launch a new
high-end line.
我們公司即將推出一系列新的高級產品。

limited edition
限量版 / 限量商品

This is the limited edition.
We have only two left on stuck.
這是限量商品，我們也只剩兩個存貨了！

其它日常生活中會用到的美式口語 Chapter **4**

gorgeous [ˋgɔrdʒəs] 絕美的 / 華麗的

The leading lady of the movie looks gorgeous
at the movie premiere.
那部電影的女主角在電影首映時看起來絕美豔麗。

小補帖 **amazing** [əˋmezɪŋ] 令人驚豔的

小補帖 **elegant** [ˋɛləgənt] 高雅的

小補帖 **classic** [ˋklæsɪk] 經典的

dress up 盛裝打扮

Everyone dresses up for this event.
大家都為了這個活動盛裝打扮。

dress down 穿著不適當

shabby [ˋʃæbɪ] 簡陋的 / 寒酸的

This lobby is too shabby for a 5-star hotel.
以五星級飯店來說，這個大廳太簡陋了。

attend [əˋtɛnd] 出席

Dr. Wilson is attending a medical conference this weekend.
威爾森博士週末要參加一場醫學研討會。

create [krɪˋet] 創造

He created a new taste of hot chocolate and his customers like it.
他研發了一種新口感的熱巧克力，他的客戶都很喜歡。

entrance [ˋɛntrəns] 入口

The entrance is on the other side.
入口在另一邊。

小補帖 **invent** [ɪnˋvɛnt] 發明

Edison invented light bulb.
愛迪生發明了燈泡。

小補帖 **as a matter of fact** 事實上

As a matter of fact, I am not buying it.
事實上，我不相信!（口語說法）

其它日常生活中會用到的美式口語 Chapter **4**

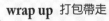

everyday needs 日常必需品 / 生活機能

Is this location convenient for general everyday needs?

這個地點的生活機能方便嗎？

retail store 雜貨零售店

註 單品購買量較少，購買者多為一般民眾，如：家樂福

wholesale store 量販店

註 單品購買量較大量，如：Costo

pharmacy [ˋfɑrməsɪ] / **drug store** 藥局

註 亦為規模不那麼大且附有藥局的零售店，如：屈臣氏

department store 百貨公司

up 的用法

What have you been up to lately?

你最近在忙什麼？

Up to you.

你決定就好。 / 悉聽尊便。

Are you up for a ride?

你想要去騎車兜兜風嗎？

shopping mall 購物商場

Stand up! 站起來！

wrap up 打包帶走

outlet [ˋaʊtˌlɛt]
過季商品折扣拍賣場

學習完本單元的單字及用語後，趕緊來做些練習，加深印象。

❶ Which means you can have the high-end design with _____ prices?

意思就是，你可以用負擔得起的價格買到高級設計師的設計？

❷ A night out in Brooklyn, huh? I _____ _____ _____ it!

好耶，布魯克林一夜遊！我要去！

❸ Wow! You look _____ ! Are you going out?

哇！你看起來超正，你要出去嗎？

❹ The leading lady of the movie looks _____ at the movie premiere.

那部電影的女主角在電影首映時看起來絕美豔麗。

❺ Is this location convenient for general _____ _____ ?

這個地點的生活機能方便嗎？

❻ Dr. Wilson is _____ a medical conference this weekend.

威爾森博士週末要參加一場醫學研討會。

❼ No invitation needed! Go _____ yourself _____ !

不需要邀請函啊！你趕快去打扮一下。

❽ This is the _____ _____ . We have only two left on stuck.

這是限量商品，我們也只剩兩個存貨了！

❾ Shall we _____ _____ now?

那我們現在可以進去一探究竟了嗎？

❿ We have _____ _____ on the front rack.

我們的新產品都在前面的架上。

解答

1. affordable 2. am up for 3. stunning 4. gorgeous
5. everyday needs 6. attending 7. dress / up
8. limited edition 9. dig in 10. new arrivals

現場看棒球比賽最熱血！

Day 29　學習量：單字50個 / 會話用語45則

到洋基棒球場（Yankee Stadium）看現場的棒球比賽

洋基球場搬好家了，更大、更豪華！藍鳥對洋基之夜，怎能錯過？凱莉邀艾凡一起去看比賽，但卻讓艾凡陷入兩難……

MP3 29

Do you like baseball?

Of course! I've been playing baseball since I was 7.

凱莉：你喜歡棒球嗎？
艾凡：當然啊！我從七歲就打棒球打到現在。

Okay! Let's cut to the chase! Blue Jays vs. Yankees,7 p.m. Are you in?

Oh, no... Kari, you have put me in a very difficult situation.

凱莉：那好！那我就直接切入重點囉，藍鳥對洋基，今天晚上七點！要不要去看？
艾凡：噢……不會吧！凱莉，你讓我很為難！

Why? Better offer?

No, my English assignment is due tomorrow. I was planning to work on that all night.

凱莉：怎麼了？有別人提供更好的約會？
艾凡：不是啦！我的英文報告明天要交，我本來打算整晚都要做報告的。

Oh, in that case you should focus on your study. I'll go with Jamie.

Don't even think about that. I'll be ready in 5 minutes.

凱莉：這樣的話，那你好好唸書，我跟潔美一起去好了！
艾凡：想都別想！我五分鐘之內準備好。

單字說明 ❶ 直接切入重點 ❷ vs. = versus 對抗 ❸ 除了當「為什麼？」，在此亦做為「怎麼了？」❹ 作業 ❺ 那樣的話 ❻ 專心於

凱莉：我們先買點食物和啤酒吧！你喜歡熱狗和雞柳條嗎？
艾凡：我都可以。

凱莉：我們的位置到了！這個球場真大。
艾凡：可不是？我的夢想成真了，我真的親眼看到美國大聯盟的比賽！

凱莉：快站起來，他們在播放美國國歌「星條旗永不落」。

 單字說明

❶ 雞柳條（因為雞柳條的形狀像手指，所以叫做 chicken fingers）

❷ 我們到了！（也可以當作「到家了；到站了」）

艾凡：（嘆氣）我真希望我可以看王建
民比賽。

小姐：不好意思，你好像坐到我的位置了。我
的位置是十三排二號。
凱莉：你的位置也是在232A區嗎？

小姐：噢！是我搞錯了，我是在309區！不好意思打擾你了！
凱莉：不用在意！對了！你的帽子很好看。

（觀眾開始鼓譟）
艾凡：天吶，你有看到那個雙殺嗎？
凱莉：加油！再來一個安打我們就有機會逆轉了。

  ❶ 嘆氣 ❷ 希望（通常表示不可能的希望，動詞接過去式） ❸ 是我的錯（口語用法） ❹ 區
❺ 別在意 ❻ 歡呼／鼓譟／打氣 ❼ 雙殺

一定要知道的單字及用語！

跟著Kari和Ivan逛完洋基棒球場後，
別忘了繼續學習其它與本單元相關的道地美語常用單字及用語！

second base (man)
二壘（手）

base path
兩壘間之路

baseball diamond (field) 棒球場

pitcher [`pɪtʃɚ]
投手

third base (man)
三壘（手）

first base (man)
一壘（手）

home base (plate)
本壘

batter [`bætɚ]
打擊手

base [bes] 壘包

plate (head) umpire
主審裁判

mitt [`mɪt] / **glove** [glʌv]
兩指手套

小補帖 **American League** 美國聯盟

小補帖 **Rookie of the Year** 年度新人王

小補帖 **Most Valuable Player (MVP)** 最有價值球員

bat [bæt] 球棒

home run / homer 全壘打

小補帖 one-base hit 一壘安打

小補帖 two-base hit 二壘安打

小補帖 three-base hit 三壘安打

小補帖 hit [hɪt] 安打

小補帖 hit- and- run 打帶跑

小補帖 wild pitch 暴投

fumble [ˋfʌmbl̩]
漏接

sliding catch
滑地接球

base on balls (four balls) / walk
四壞球 / 保送

小補帖 intentional walk 故意四壞球

小補帖 ball [bɔl] 壞球

小補帖 strike [straɪk] 好球　小補帖 fielding [fildɪŋ] 守備

strike zone 好球帶

sacrifice fly 高飛犧牲打

pinch hitter 代打

sacrifice hit 犧牲打

game ball 勝利紀念球

fair ball 界內球

foul ball 界外球

high fly ball 高飛球

steal 盜壘

ground ball 滾地球

tip [tɪp] 擦棒球

double play 雙殺

triple play 三殺

check [tʃɛk] 牽制

control [kən`trol] 控球

inning [ˋɪnɪŋ] 局

extra inning 延長（局）

left on base 殘壘數

Chapter 4
其它日常生活中會用到的美式口語

來做練習吧！Let's practice

學習完本單元的單字及用語後，趕緊來做些練習，加深印象。

① Oh, _____ _____ . Mine is in section 309. Sorry to bother you.

噢！是我搞錯了，我是在309區！不好意思打擾你了！

② _____ _____ ! Nice hat by the way.

不用在意！對了！你的帽子很好看。

③ Okay! Let's _____ _____ _____ _____ !

那好！那我就直接切入重點囉。

④ Why? Better _____ ?

怎麼了？有別人提供更好的約會？

⑤ Oh, _____ _____ _____ you should focus on your study. I'll go with Jamie.

這樣的話，那你好好唸書，我跟潔美一起去好了！

⑥ How about hot dogs and _____ _____ ?

你喜歡熱狗和雞柳條嗎？

⑦ No, my English _____ is due tomorrow.

不是啦！我的英文報告明天要交

⑧ _____ ball

界外球

⑨ _____ ball

界內球

⑩ Most _____ Player

最有價值球員

解答

1. my bad 2. Never mind 3. cut to the chase 4. offer
5. in that case 6. chicken fingers 7. assigment 8. foul
9. fair 10. Valuable

國家圖書館出版品預行編目資料

說出美國人的每一天——連英文老師都在學的
「道地口語美語」／Kerra Tsai 著.
-- 初版.-- 臺北市：易富文化, 2011.08
　面；　公分

ISBN　978-986-6224-55-3（平裝附光碟片）
1. 英語 2. 口語 3. 會話

805.188　　　　　　　　　　100012141

說出
美國人的
每一天
連英文老師都在學的「道地口語美語」

書名 / 說出美國人的每一天——連英文老師都在學的「道地口語美語」

作者 / Kerra Tsai

發行人 / 蔣敬祖

副總經理 / 陳弘毅

總編輯 / 常祈天

執行編輯 / 蔣勤曜・劉俐伶

美術編輯 / 彭君如

內文插畫・排版 / 夢想國工作室

法律顧問 / 北辰著作權事務所蕭雄淋律師

印製 / 源順印刷有限公司

初版 / 2011年08月

出版 / 我識出版集團——懶鬼子英日語

電話 / （02）2345-7222

傳真 / （02）2345-5758

地址 / 台北市忠孝東路五段372巷27弄78之1號1樓

郵政劃撥 / 19793190

戶名 / 我識出版社

網路書店 / www.17buy.com.tw

網路客服Email / iam.group@17buy.com.tw

定價 / 新台幣349 元 / 港幣116 元 （附1MP3）

總經銷 / 創智文化有限公司

地址 / 新北市土城區忠承路89號6樓

港澳總經銷 / 和平圖書有限公司

地址 / 香港柴灣嘉業街12號百樂門大廈17樓

電話 / (852)2804-6687　傳真 / (852)2804-6409

懒鬼子 英日語
Language
17buy.com.tw

懶鬼子 英日語
Language
17buy.com.tw